William C. Johnson graduated from the University of Kansas with a degree in advertising, then served as an officer in the Navy during Vietnam War. He started his career as a copywriter at Look Magazine, then joined Fingerhut, a catalog retailer, eventually becoming chairman and CEO. After that, he was recruited to a children's book publishing company, Grolier, as chairman and CEO, and finished his business career working with Freeman Spogli, a private equity firm. Mr. Johnson lives in Rancho Santa Fe, California, with his wife, Fran, and visits his two kids and five grandchildren as often as possible.

William C. Johnson

SHIRA

AUSTIN MACAULEY PUBLISHERS™

LONDON • CAMBRIDGE • NEW YORK • SHARJAH

Ordering Information
Quantity sales: Special discounts are available on quantity purchases by corporations, associations, and others. For details, contact the publisher at the address below.

Publisher's Cataloging-in-Publication data
Johnson, William C.
Shira

ISBN 9781685624170 (Paperback)
ISBN 9781685624194 (ePub e-book)
ISBN 9781685624187 (Audiobook)

Library of Congress Control Number: 2022922292

www.austinmacauley.com/us

First Published 2023
Austin Macauley Publishers LLC
40 Wall Street, 33rd Floor, Suite 3302
New York, NY 10005
USA

mail-usa@austinmacauley.com
+1 (646) 5125767

I want to thank Van and Jeanne Hoisington, Dick and Clara Kennedy, my sister, Rusty Trenary, my son, Scott, a published author in his own right, his wife, Erin, and my daughter, A.J. Czerwinski, for their unwavering support of my writing efforts.

And, most of all, my loving wife, Fran, who lived through many versions of *Shira*, guiding me and the story to what I hope is a successful conclusion.

Introduction

As the waiter passes out the menus, he's surprised at how quickly the mood of the four men has changed.

Once somber and business-like as they pored over documents at a back table of the *Le Meridian* hotel restaurant, they are now flushed and happy.

Their business papers, so important a few minutes before, have disappeared into briefcases, replaced by linen tablecloths, several cut glass carafes filled with fine red wine, and elegant place settings of polished silverware.

They are all laughing and making toasts, seemingly oblivious to the others dining around them.

One of the men, an elegant-looking Arab, seems to be in charge, and not only is he drinking more than the others, he's gesturing and talking more as well. The other three men listen intently, occasionally nodding and raising their glasses in agreement.

Then, when the dinner and festivities are over, all four men rise, shake hands, and briefcases in hand, leave the table, all headed in different directions.

Two stride across the lobby and exit through the main doors. Another goes directly to the elevator bank and pushes the "up" arrow, apparently heading to his room. For him, the evening is over.

But, for the leader of the group, it isn't. Not just yet.

He heads directly for the bar. Or maybe not so directly, as he carefully weaves his way through the tables, his legs as wobbly as a sailor's on the high seas.

Near the front of the restaurant, the man passes a couple of young women seated alone at a table for four. They both look up and smile at him, something that doesn't happen very often to the middle-aged Egyptian. But discretion being the better part of valor, the man moves on toward the bar in search of a nightcap.

One of the women rises and follows him.

An hour or so later, the distinguished Arab, Yahia el-Mashad, is found stabbed to death in his hotel room.

It turns out he's the scientist in charge of the entire Iraqi nuclear program, and the Mossad is rumored to have caused his death.

Chapter 1
Paris

The structure is impressive, and so characteristic of Shira Adelson's newly adopted city.

Its wide, four-legged, base squats on the ground as firmly as Parisians hold on to their past. The wrought-iron lattice work at the top of the tower tapers up a thousand feet to a slim needle-like protuberance, symbolically pointing skyward, toward the bright future that was envisioned for France in the late 1880's when the tower was built.

Yes, it is beautiful, Shira admits to herself, *but it is arrogant as well. The delicate lacy design and the gracefulness of its lines are aesthetically pleasing, but they convey an icy haughtiness, much like the Parisians I've met. The structure is visible anywhere in the city, and seems to shout—I'm the Eiffel Tower and you are not.*

"Shira, you're not listening," Mort Adelson says. "I asked about your grades."

The father and daughter are having their normal Saturday lunch at a surprisingly ordinary brassiere whose best feature is its proximity to the Eiffel Tower.

To Shira, however, the location doesn't make up for the undercooked pasta and bland sauce that the two of them are pushing around on their plates.

If truth be told, Shira would rather be doing almost anything other than sitting here, answering her father's intrusive questions.

But, since the divorce, spending Saturdays with him has been her lot in life. She realizes, of course, that her situation is not unique but, to her mind, nobody's divorced father can possibly be the boor hers is. A thought undoubtedly shared by millions of teenagers.

"I'm sorry. I was admiring the tower, father. What did you say?"

"Your C in mathematics," Mr. Adelson says. "What are we going to do about that?"

What are we going to do about it? she thinks. *Well, maybe you could do my homework. Or maybe you could meet my teacher and tell her how archaic her teaching is. Or maybe you could take my place, cram your fat ass into the small hardwood desk chair, and see if you can stay awake while that scarecrow of a crone drones on about arithmetic equations, or some such.*

But, instead, Shira says, "We're going to study more, father. We're going to work harder, and make a really special effort to get that C up to a B before our final grades come out. That's what we are going to do, father."

Then, she smiles sweetly at him, knowing full well how her sarcasm stings. But she also knows that her father won't challenge her, not if he wants these weekly visits to continue.

She looks back at the Eiffel Tower and comments, "You know, when it was first built, many critics found it ugly. In fact, I read somewhere that one critic even ate lunch in it every day just so he wouldn't have to look at it."

"Hard to believe," Mr. Adelson says.

"Maybe he just didn't want to eat in this place," Shira replies, pushing her half-eaten plate of cold pasta away.

Mr. Adelson says nothing, which he learned long ago was the safest way to deal with Shira's tart tongue.

And her mother's as well.

Shira and her parents moved to Paris about five years ago from Haifa, Israel. Within a year, she had acclimated quite well but her parents had not. Her mother and father argued about everything; their neighborhood, their friends, their money, and how to raise their daughter. Eventually, they separated, and then divorced, something Shira welcomed at the time.

Some kids might have blamed themselves for causing their parents to split but not Shira. To her mind, they were an incredible mismatch from the beginning, and any role she played in the divorce was more heroic than tragic.

And she was probably right. The Adelsons seem much happier now but that isn't important to Shira. Like most teenagers, what's important is that she's happy.

And she is.

She loves the freedom that their divorce has afforded her, and the power. She's certainly made the most of it, working one parent against the other whenever possible.

In her mind Shira has become an independent woman, or at least as independent as a 15-year-old can be.

The problem in her parents' ill-fated relationship is that, like Shira, her mother happens to be a free spirit that her father never learned to control. From the get-go, Chaka has pretty much done whatever she wanted.

In fact, she was the one who chose to move to Paris, partially because it fit her mood at the time, but also because she could. Since Mort had been caught cheating on Chaka several times, he had little say in the matter. And Shira welcomed the move, seeing it as a way to become even more independent.

She was right. In the laissez-faire, 1960's ambience of Paris, Shira has really blossomed. Even with her C in math, she's done well in school, much of it because she speaks French fluently, something that, to this point, has eluded her parents.

In fact, because of that, and because of a certain savoir-faire that she's picked up along the way, Shira seems more French than Jewish, and to the untrained eye, could be just another young, spoiled, flirty Parisian girl who thinks the world owes her something.

But, in truth, Shira is nothing like that.

The Six-Day War in June, 1967 changed Israel; yes, but it also changed her. For the very first time, she had to come to grips with how Jewish she is, and how vulnerable.

Shira now realizes that she can no longer be the wide-eyed, carefree teenager she was when she arrived in Paris, happily exploring its superficial pleasures without regard to her own safety.

No, the war has made her more wary, and more introspective, and more frightened. She realizes that she needs to take charge of her life, and become less dependent on others. Especially her parents. Also, though few would suspect it from looking at her, the war has made Shira more Jewish as well.

So, when her French high school fling is over, she plans to return to Israel, with the ultimate goal of protecting, and strengthening, her very fragile new country.

Bottom-line, Shira is determined to get her B in math, maybe even an A, not because her father wants her to, but because she needs to.

She now sees her grades as her ticket out of Paris, away from her parents, away from the Eiffel Tower, and also away from the frivolous French lifestyle that she has learned to abhor over the last few years.

****

"Move around, Shira. Have fun. Flip your hair," photographer Jacques Lamont says in French to the 17-year-old girl who is trying her best to do what he wants.

"Don't pose," he continues, "Just be yourself, carefree, uninhibited. Don't force it. The camera will find you."

Jacques met Shira through one of his friends. He was struck immediately by her exotically dark beauty.

She has everything it takes to be a successful model, he told himself at the time. *A unique face with porcelain skin, framed by silky brown hair, and a mysterious half-smile, like the Mona Lisa, only more beautiful.*

What's more, the camera adores her. And she doesn't have a bad feature, or angle, that he needs to work around.

Shira looks like a lot of young girls in Paris, yes, but with an intelligence in her dark brown eyes that few others have. Maybe it's because of her heritage. Or her life experiences. But she has a maturity and melancholy about her that the camera loves.

She also has an ability to change her mood on demand, just by raising an eyebrow or curling her lip. In fact, Jacques has never known a girl so young who can vary her appearance so easily. She can look fifteen or twenty-five, or even thirty-five, if she needs to. She can appear to be ordinary or aristocratic, angry or inviting, cold or coquettish, and it's clear to Jacques that, in Shira, he has uncovered a rare modeling talent.

But it's also obvious to him that Shira isn't that comfortable in front of the camera.

She's always aware of it, where it is. And she's a bit stilted in her movements, seemingly over-worried about what she looks like, although, for the life of him, Jacques can't understand why.

It isn't just that she's self-conscious, which is entirely normal for anybody the first session. It's more that she's too aware, or too wary, of everything going on around her. A little jumpy at times, and even scared, as if the camera is a gun about to go off.

"This isn't that serious," Jacques says to her, trying to calm her down. "It's not life or death."

But he doesn't understand that, with Shira, everything is life or death, and that, no matter how much potential she may have as a model, she's already decided never to step in front of a camera again.

****

Mort and Chaka Adelson are together for the first time since their divorce. They are seated in the first row of the impressive Lycée Saint-Louis auditorium, well-dressed, stony-faced, and anxiously awaiting their daughter's graduation ceremony.

Founded as the College d'Harcourt in 1280, and housed in a white French colonial building on boulevard Saint-Michel since 1814, Lycée Saint-Louis is one of the most important prep schools in all of Europe.

Shira is fortunate to have been accepted in the first place, to have excelled in a highly competitive academic environment, and to be graduating today, not only with honors, but also as the only student asked to represent her class and give a short speech.

She will be speaking in French, of course, rather than her native Hebrew. Therefore, her parents are able to understand her, but just barely because their French is conversational while hers is perfect Parisian, beautiful, intricate, and evocative, without the trace of an accent.

Given that she knew nobody when she arrived, Shira's tenure at Lycée Saint Louis has been highly successful, not only in the classroom but also outside it. And although she's had few really close friends through the years, Shira has always been well-liked, by the girls, yes, but even more by the boys. In fact, in her last two years here, she's had a succession of boyfriends, all of whom she casually discarded when the relationship got too cloying for her.

Now, with her high school finally behind her, she's glad that she's free to forge her own way, without the added hassle of a romantic relationship.

When Shira rises to speak, Mort nervously grabs Chaka's hand and surprisingly, she returns his firm grip. Whatever their differences in the past, they've always been solidly behind their gifted daughter, although, when apart, each takes full credit for her success.

"I want to start by thanking all of those sitting here who contributed to my success and that of my fellow students," Shira begins, in perfect French.

Then, she names each teacher, administrator, and counselor that has helped her, by name, giving one or two, often humorous, anecdotes about them. She describes their best traits and what she learned from each.

Shira talks about fellow students and how they inspired or assisted her, and she even compliments the curriculum she was offered, except for math, the concepts of which still elude her, she says. She talks about some of the school's distinguished graduates, and how they impacted the course of world events. And she closes by promising to do the school proud and hoping that, someday, another graduate will mention her in their speech, not because she's famous or infamous, but because she's accomplished something that really has made a difference in the world.

Then, she sits down to a standing ovation.

Shira has said nothing about her parents. But that isn't the worst part for Mort and Chaka. When she finally reaches them, through the throngs of well-wishers, Shira rudely informs them that she isn't accepting the scholarship to the Sorbonne as they had been led to believe.

Instead, she is going back to Israel, alone, to enroll at the Hebrew University of Jerusalem.

She's over them, she tells them coldly, and she's over their frivolous dalliance with France as well. Now, eighteen years old with a high school degree, Shira is eager to get on with her real life, whatever that might be.

Chapter 2
Jerusalem

Shira Adelson's real life, as she describes it, is finally beginning in Jerusalem. She's decided to attend Hebrew University because, like the Jewish people, it has a rich, albeit troubled, past. Since the school's opening in 1925, there have been a number of significant military and terrorist attacks against the university, and control of it has shifted from the Jews to the Arabs and, after the war in 1967, back to the Jews again. What better place for her to learn about her country and her roots?

It is only two years after the Six-Day-War has ended and Shira is surprised to find a campus much like one she might find anywhere. The main campus tumbles over, and around the base of Mount Scopus, a location that, because of its unobstructed views of the city, has always been important militarily. But, with its lightly forested environs, and recently-renovated white granite buildings, the campus is now a beautiful and bucolic oasis overlooking a city still unsettled and dangerous.

Shira sees nothing to remind her of the senseless violence that has occurred here over the decades and is surprised to find the campus not scary at all, but inviting and alive with hope and anticipation. It literally buzzes with energy as students hustle from one place to another; moving into new quarters, signing up for classes, meeting other students, exactly the way it might be at any other university in the world.

Still, for Shira, although the campus doesn't really frighten her, the forced social interactions on a college campus make her uncomfortable. She isn't a naturally outgoing person and here, her reluctance to immediately engage with people is a handicap. She feels more alone than she did with her French friends in Paris and wonders if she made the right choice, choosing Hebrew University over the Sorbonne.

To complicate things, because she didn't grow up in Israel, Shira has no ready-made friends here to help her ease into college life. Nor any shared experiences on which to build friendships. And for the first time in her life, she feels utterly alone.

When people ask her where she's from, she says Paris, and her answer elicits mixed reactions. Some are jealous. Others categorize her immediately as a snob. But most don't think about her at all. They just pass her by quickly, making a mental note to avoid her, like they would any other alien being.

At one point, her loneliness gets so bad that she longs for the tedious lunches with her dad. At least, he could provide some social stimulation for her, albeit mostly one-sided and inane. Even that would be better than nothing.

Fortunately, that mood passes quickly and over time, her blossoming beauty begins to attract male attention. She goes out on a few dates. Then, through them, meets some girls she likes, and slowly begins to put together the semblance of a social life.

In the classroom, Shira is significantly more successful than she is socially. She finds that her interest in most subjects, no matter how arcane they might be, is more than other students, and her willingness to work is unmatched.

Slowly, her social life takes a back seat to her studies, and Shira quickly rises to the top of every class, further limiting her ability to make new friends.

Everything she learns, however, fuels her patriotism. While her parents hid their background, Shira embraces her Jewish roots, loudly, and often. And here in the symbolic center of the Arab-Israeli conflict, her patriotic feelings coalesce, and her suppressed anger smolders.

In her sophomore year, Shira finds a soulmate.

Aaron Schwartz is good-looking, smart and, like her, patriotic. On their first date, even at the risk of it being their last, the two of them discuss politics and religion.

Their opinions don't mesh exactly but their differences are the fodder for many late-night discussions. In fact, Shira often wakes up in the middle of the night with a thought that she wants to express to Aaron. Most often she holds it until they next get together, but occasionally, no matter how late, she calls him to discuss whatever is on her mind, sometimes until the sun rises.

Aaron is good for Shira. And although her circle of friends has shrunk considerably, she's never lonely.

In fact, it's surprising how much one person, or more appropriately, one highly active mind, can keep her totally engaged. An hour spent with Aaron is worth hundreds of hours spent with her shallow and vapid girlfriends.

And the sex is terrific, too. When a particularly enlightening discussion takes place, leading to new insights for Shira, she likes to cap it off by making love.

Surprisingly, perhaps, Shira has become the aggressor in the relationship. Some might think that she's addicted to the sex, but actually, it's kind of the opposite. The intellectual discovery process stimulates her brain, and the other parts of her body naturally follow. In a way, her mind, or maybe Aaron's, is the aphrodisiac that makes their sex so wonderful.

Also, Shira has begun to explore another addiction. She's always been a risk-taker, something that worried her parents through the years. But, now, with her growing freedom, her unlocked feelings, and her proximity to danger, she's begun to ratchet things up a notch.

Despite its history, Hebrew University is a relatively safe place these days but nobody could say that about Jerusalem, especially at night. And, for a Jewish girl like Shira, some sections are way more dangerous than others.

Take the Muslim Quarter, for example. No students go there, partially because they're afraid to, but also because there's nothing there to interest them. No bands, no bars, and no other students.

So, naturally, being the nonconformist she is, and a dare-devil to boot, Shira decides she has to go there, and she convinces Aaron to join her.

They go on a Saturday, after their mid-day meal, with the intention to just look around a bit before it gets too dark.

They park outside the Damascus Gate, and Shira explains to Aaron that the gate is so-named because back in the day, you could take your camels, go straight out the gate, onto the road, and without turning at all, eventually, reach Damascus.

"But we have no camels," he replies.

"Same with the Jaffa Gate," she says, ignoring his remark.

The road going out through it leads straight to Jaffa, and in Shira's mind, although that gate is a much safer place for a Jew to enter the Muslim Quarter, at this stage of her life she prefers the road less traveled.

So, Shira and Aaron choose the Damascus Gate and stroll through it, arm in arm, heads held high, driven by the ignorance and optimism of youth.

Shira is plainly-dressed and intelligent enough to have left her Jewish star necklace back at the dormitory. Likewise, Aaron is pretty nondescript in his black turtle-neck and unpressed blue jeans.

Fortunately, nobody seems to pay them much attention. They stroll through the cobble-stone streets, stopping at booths along the way to look at handiworks, clothing, and even fresh food stocks. Just like tourists.

Eventually feeling more confident, Shira and Aaron stop at a cheese shop to sample kunefe, a very sweet cheese delicacy sold in Muslim marketplaces around the world. It doesn't taste like anything Shira has eaten before and she jokes to Aaron that, for her, it's an acquired taste that she would rather not acquire.

As they wander around the unfamiliar neighborhood and dusk settles in, Aaron and Shira get more adventurous. Instead of leaving before sundown, as originally planned, they stop at a tiny neighborhood cafe that has only two tables out front. The perfect place for an amorous couple who just want to be left alone.

Looking at the barely comprehensible menu briefly, they order two glasses of Sauvignon Blanc and two bowls of siniyeh, a kind of seasoned stew that the waiter says is popular in Muslim villages. It turns out to be delicious and filling. So far, so good.

However, as they finish up their meal, two young boys start hovering around their table. Then, they're joined by two more. All have surly looks on their faces. None of them look at Aaron and Shira directly but they're certainly invading the couple's space in a way that's very uncomfortable.

To make matters worse, the cafe proprietors have closed the door to their restaurant, leaving the two tables outside unattended.

"This can't be good," Aaron whispers to Shira as he tosses a few bills on the table. They exchange knowing glances, calmly rise, and holding hands, start to run.

One boy follows them briefly but the others are distracted by the cash, and after running only a few steps, the lone pursuer decides to go back as well to claim his share.

Shira and Aaron are left alone, half-running and half-stumbling their way toward the Damascus Gate. The cobblestones are a problem but not nearly the problem that their laughing is.

Eventually, they can go no further. The two of them stop short of the gate, hearts pounding, hands on knees, and double over, guffawing, with tears running down their cheeks.

They are strangely amused by their harrowing escape, and decide right then and there that they will return to the Muslim section of Jerusalem often, if only for the laughs.

****

The Hebrew University of Jerusalem is noted for both its pre- and post-medical programs.

There are five affiliated teaching hospitals connected to the university, the most infamous being the Hadassah Medical School, a target of Arab military operations in both the 1948 War and the Six-Day War in 1967.

Primarily because of that hospital, the curriculum at Hebrew University is among the best in the world for wannabe medical students, and Shira has taken full advantage of the opportunity. She has excellent grades and her admission to medical school after college is a forgone conclusion. Her ultimate goal is to practice in Jerusalem, a city she has come to love.

So, with that career in mind, Shira has also been taking an Arabic language course, focused primarily on the dialects spoken in her now-chosen home city. Gifted in languages anyway, Shira is now fluent in her native Hebrew, French, English, and Arabic.

Given her focus on her studies, Shira's romance with Aaron has been an on and off affair the last two years. They still date periodically but the relationship is nowhere near as intense as it was in the beginning.

In fact, the debates that energized both of them before, have now, for Shira at least, become a bit tiresome.

Philosophically, they often differ. And they have more trouble than before finding common ground.

Politically, they have drifted apart as well. In their discussions, Aaron challenges many of the moves the Israeli government is making and assigns some blame for the troubled Middle East situation to Prime Minister Yitzhak Begin and his Labor Party.

Shira, on the other hand, is more tolerant of her government's actions and increasingly suspicious of the peace offerings made by Anwar Sadat and other Arab leaders. The couple's debates are still healthy but any agreement is much more elusive than it had been before. And as might be expected, their political differences have affected their lovemaking.

Shira continues to attract other suitors, and elects to accept an invite every now and then, but so far, none have proven interesting enough to take Aaron's place.

Still, she keeps looking and so, when she gets an unexpected offer to have coffee with a good-looking guy in her chemistry class, she doesn't hesitate.

On her way to meet him her expectations are high. She is excited at the prospect of finding the guy who might help her forget about Aaron once and for all. But, when she arrives, her date isn't there alone, eagerly waiting for her, as she had hoped.

Instead, he's there with another, much older man. Maybe a professor. Probably with tenure. Lots of tenure. And sporting a craggy face, bespectacled eyes, and baggy wrinkled clothes. His looks are in sharp contrast to the handsome, well-dressed student sitting next to him. And everything about the old man shouts ordinary.

Shira's confused about what he's doing here, on her date, with her new boyfriend-to-be. Then, she becomes even more confused. Surprisingly, and unfortunately, after introducing his companion as a friend named Ari Lavon, the good-looking guy gets up, wishes Shira all the best, and exits, leaving her alone with the stranger.

Certainly not what she had planned.

"Miss Adelson, I'm pleased to meet you," Ari says. "We've been following your career for a long time."

"My career? Really? What career?" she answers. "And who's we?"

"Well, for now, let's just say the Israeli government," the man answers.

A number of possibilities run through Shira's head, none of them good. She doesn't know the guy who left, which is too bad. And she doesn't know this man either. Nor does she want to. He's old enough to be her grandfather.

What the hell could he want with me? she thinks. *If he's government, I must be in some kind of trouble. But it may be even worse if he's not.*

"Can I see some identification, please?" she asks.

"That's not the way it works," he replies.

"I don't care how it works," Shira says rising from her seat. "It was nice meeting you, Mr. Lavon. But I need to get to class."

"Mossad."

"What?" she replies.

"I'm Mossad," he repeats rather meekly, in a high voice. "And we're not used to showing identification."

Shira stares into the man's eyes, looking for some sign that he's lying, or kidding, or anything other than actually being a member of the most notorious spy organization in the world. But she sees nothing. He's stone-faced.

Ira goes on, "You'll learn why we don't show identification when you join our organization."

"I'm not joining your organization. Not for a million dollars, sir. I'm going to be a doctor and save lives, not take them," Shira responds, and walks away, hoping never to see Mr. Lavon again.

But the old Mossad spymaster knows better. He'll just bide his time.

****

Hadassah Ein Karem Hospital is a place of learning and healing. Shira Adelson is planning to do a lot of both.

Every kind of person imaginable comes into this hospital and regardless of their color, religion, or race, they all get wheeled into the same trauma center to be treated by whatever medical staff is available at the time. By definition, their treatments should be agnostic.

Terrorist or victim, it shouldn't matter to the care-givers. The attending doctor or nurse may be Arab or Jewish or even Catholic or Protestant but their religious or political views aren't really relevant here. All that matters is how well-trained they are, and at this hospital, they're among the best in the world.

Shira could be a good example of that, except for one thing. Her passion for Israel and her fellow countrymen, still glows brightly, just beneath the surface. So, when she helps nurse a young Arab back to health, it's probably better that she not know that he's a failed suicide bomber, as an example. Or that, if his bomb hadn't malfunctioned, he would have killed dozens of Jews.

Unfortunately, situations like that aren't unique here. For decades, this hospital has been at the epicenter of what is truly a war. This city is a battleground in that war and the carnage created by Arab terrorist activities is all around her and because of that, she sees herself as a war victim too. She is an angry young woman.

Aaron is still in her life but just barely. After graduation, he told her he joined an Arab outreach group dedicated to improving relationships in Jerusalem and the Gaza Strip, something Shira can't imagine doing. Especially when she's exposed daily to the savagery of their enemies.

He lives near the hospital but travels a lot, so getting together is even harder than solving a Rubik's cube. And convenience being a necessary part of romance these days, Shira has begun to hang out with a fellow medical student that she likes but certainly doesn't love.

He's a surprisingly optimistic fellow, with an offbeat sense of humor that suits her mood perfectly. In fact, if it wasn't for his "gallows" humor, she would find it harder to cope with the ungodly hours and emotional impact of what they do day in and day out.

His name is Howard Goldstein, and he isn't much to look at. Only slightly taller than Shira, he has a droopy face that reminds her of a Basset Hound. His doughy, dead-pan look serves as a perfect foil for a rapier-like wit that seemingly comes out of nowhere.

His humor is particularly effective, not just because it's so unexpected, but also because most have to think about it for a second, which gives it more impact.

Howard invites people into his twisted world and those that take the trouble to come in are often richly rewarded. Not that Howard cares whether they are or not. He'll say or do anything, the quirkier the better, without regard to how it's received. Just so it's funny.

Shira appreciates Howard's insouciance and his way with words and his one-liners. Like, "There hasn't been a prayer invented that could save this guy's soul." Or, "There's nothing about her face that a traffic accident wouldn't cure."

Always dark. always cutting. Always funny. Well, maybe not always. But, often enough.

Sometimes, at the most inopportune times, Shira remembers something that Howard said earlier and chuckles aloud, drawing strange looks from the people working around her.

Although Shira is drawn to Howard because he entertains her, to call their relationship a romance would be grossly overstating the situation.

For one thing, they don't go out on normal dates, which, of course, wouldn't work into their schedules very well anyway. Instead, they might meet at the cafeteria vending machines for a sandwich or soda, or just grab a middle-of-the-night coffee. And, sometimes, between classes, they just run into each other by accident, and find two available chairs to sit down, and talk.

In the beginning, the relationship is purely platonic, built on mutual interests and sarcastic banter. But slowly it graduates to a sexual one, not like what Shira enjoyed with Aaron, of course, but satisfying nonetheless.

The two students grab their pleasure wherever they can. Once, after giving a patient a nightly sleeping pill, Howard and Shira don't leave the room. Instead, they wait until the patient is asleep, then, slip into an adjacent vacant bed and make love, their passion fueled by the risk and danger. Fortunately, the patient never wakes up and nobody else walks in on them.

Given the disparity between Shira's cool and striking appearance, and Howard's sorta dumpy one, few would believe that there's anything sexual or romantic going on between them, and by unspoken agreement, the two medical students are happy to keep up that charade.

There are no outward displays of affection, no winks or knowing smiles. To the eye of a casual observer, they are all business. Just two young people, who are forced to be with each other, driven by the common desire to become doctors and help people.

During her second year of medical school Shira begins to question what she's doing there. The regimen is brutal, sleep rare, studies difficult, and nerves raw.

But, even worse than that, Shira wonders if being a doctor is even worth it. Her dream of having her own practice, even in a patient-rich environment like Jerusalem, is not as appealing as it once was.

That point is really hammered home when, through one of her sponsors, she meets a doctor with an office like the one she envisions for herself. Although he seems prosperous and relatively happy with his lot, Shira is struck by how closely the life he leads resembles the one she's not enjoying right now. Overly demanding patients. Mind numbing routine. Crazy hours. And, to top it all off, when the healing work is done, there's always the paperwork, and the second guessing.

Saving lives is fulfilling. Documenting it? Not so much.

Then, between classes one day, out on the quad, Shira notices an old man in glasses coming toward her, slowly and gingerly, acting as if he knows her. He looks rumpled, slightly familiar, and out-of-place on a college campus populated by students and young doctors-to-be.

Shira goes immediately into lock-down mode. Head down. Eyes straight ahead. Purposeful walk. Anything she can do to convey to the man that she's not interested in him, or whatever he's selling. She just hopes her body language is as good as the four other languages she speaks.

"Ms. Adelson, you might not remember me. I'm Ari Lavon," the unimpressive man says in a squeaky voice, ignoring the visible signs that she wants to be left alone.

He extends his hand. But Shira ignores the gesture and pushes past him, making no eye contact at all. She's determined to ignore the man, and his intrusion, no matter what he has to say.

Ari lets her pass and when she's several feet past him, her memory begins to clear. He's the guy from Mossad.

She thinks, *"What in the hell could he want?"*

Shira looks back quizzically, saying nothing.

"May I have a moment of your time?" he asks, motioning her toward a nearby bench.

****

31

Shira has now held several meetings with Ari Lavon, all at his request. He's been friendly, courteous, and persistent, determined to enlist her to join his organization.

He encourages her to "forget this doctor nonsense," as he calls it, join the Mossad, and take her rightful place on the frontlines of the decades-old war against Israel's enemies.

She's uniquely qualified, he says, to help the Mossad right away. Her language skills, medical training, and chameleon-like ability to look either stunning or incredibly ordinary, are all attributes that his organization could find useful.

As flattered as Shira is, she isn't an easy sell. To do what Ari suggests, Shira not only has to give up her original dream of being a doctor. She also has to leave all vestiges of her old life behind. Maybe even her identity.

Even worse, she has to ditch all that she's been working toward, the dream of independence, money, a comfortable life. That will all be gone. And, at least for now, she'll have to put a husband and family on the back burner as well.

The choice is clear. Be a doctor, healing people, or a spy, killing them? Not that hard a decision for any sane person.

Except—

Shira likes excitement and risk. Also, she loves her country and understands that, if somebody doesn't come to its defense, the thought of a happy, safe life is just a pipe dream anyway. There are people everywhere who think the whole concept of a Jewish State is wrong, and they won't stop until Israel is wiped off the face of the earth.

So, Shira doesn't say "no" right away. Instead, she tells Ari she will think about it, which, in his experience, is the same as saying yes. He's visibly excited.

Still, despite Ari's enthusiasm, Shira really isn't sure what she should do. She needs somebody she trusts to help her wrestle around with the decision and since she no longer has a relationship with her parents, she decides to call Aaron.

"Say that again," Aaron asks.

"I'm thinking about quitting medical school to pursue other opportunities," Shira replies. "I'm not really cut out to be a doctor."

"Are you kidding me?" Aaron counters. "You would be the perfect doctor. You're smart and you care about people."

"Not all people," she counters cryptically.

"Fair enough, but all people are entitled to top-notch medical care and nobody will be able to deliver that better than you, Shira," he argues.

"If I know a patient is a terrorist, I don't think I could let him live."

"As a doctor, that's not your decision to make, is it?" Aaron asks rhetorically.

"Exactly," Shira agrees. "And I want it to be my decision."

"What are you going to do, then?" he asks.

"I don't know yet but I'll keep you posted," she responds.

"You could help me smooth relations between Israel and our Arab adversaries."

"Not on your life."

33

Chapter 3
Tel Aviv

Yitzhak Hofi is an important and serious man.

As the Director of the Mossad, he makes all of the agency's most important decisions, like launching operations. Then, staffing them, monitoring their progress, and closing them down if necessary.

Yitzhak is solely responsible to the Prime Minister for every one of the dozens of operations run by the Mossad annually, and although most of what his people do is unknown to the public, the actual results are often highly visible, especially the failures.

Granted, Yitzhak has had enough success in his life to handle a few failures. But that doesn't mean he won't do everything he can to keep them from happening. His ability to foresee events, bad and good, and influence them, is a major reason he's in his position.

The Director first served honorably in the Palmach, an underground paramilitary group fighting for Israeli independence.

Then, after Israel became a nation, Yitzhak helped start the Israeli Defense Forces and distinguished himself as a commander during the 1973 Arab-Israeli War. In fact, he performed so well in combat that, unsurprisingly, the next year the Prime Minister appointed him to his current position as head of the Mossad.

Although fairly new to the position, Yitzhak Hofi looks the part of a seasoned spymaster. Dark-haired, full-faced, with squinty eyes and a receding hairline, he has a brooding intimidating presence. Yitzhak could play a heavy in Hollywood if he weren't already one in real life.

When Shira is led in to meet him, Yitzhak is hunched over his desk, sorting through papers, prominently marked TOP SECRET in red across the top. She stands nervously before him for several minutes, with Ari at her side, shifting her weight from one foot to the next, before the chief of spies finally looks up and acknowledges her.

"What have we here?" Yitzhak's voice booms, his dark, unblinking eyes staring right into hers.

"A new recruit," Ari Lavon replies softly. "Her name is Shira Adelson. She's been training to be a doctor but has decided she can help her country more by serving in the Mossad."

"Does she know what she's getting into?" The Director asks, still looking at Shira.

"Probably not. Does anybody, really?" Ari replies.

"I mean because she's not a he."

"She can handle herself," Ari counters, "and, frankly, there are situations in our business that a woman is far better suited to handle than a man."

Yitzhak's eyebrows rise a bit but he doesn't say anything. He just keeps glaring at her, obviously still skeptical.

Shira does her best to respond in kind, silent and expressionless. She matches him glare for glare, unwilling to back down for anyone.

"OK," he finally says, looking at Ari for the first time, "but don't waste a lot of time training her before you put her in the field. We may as well find out if she can hack it sooner rather than later."

Then, the Director goes back to his paperwork, fairly certain that he'll never see the pretty young medical student again.

But he is wrong.

After leaving the Director's office, Shira turns to Ari and asks, "What the hell was that about?"

"Don't take it personally," he answers. "We've had limited success with female agents in the past and Yitzhak's not interested in wasting any more time or resources on what he calls 'frivolous adventure seekers'."

"I'm certainly not that."

"Listen, I'm not any more sure than he is whether you're cut out for this line of work," Ari says, "but I know one thing. You're a fighter. Which is why I recruited you in the first place. And why I think you'll succeed."

"If you expect me to say thank you, don't hold your breath," Shira responds. "And anytime you think I can't make it, just let me know and you'll never see me again."

Ari is a little taken aback by the intensity of her feelings.

"But I won't quit on my own," she goes on.

"You quit trying to be a doctor," he reminds her.

"To help Israel, remember? I'll never quit on my country. You must know that."

"I do," Ari says softly.

****

Trying to be a doctor was hard for Shira, but trying to be a spy is even harder.

At least, that's how she feels at the moment, stretched out on an exercise mat, her chest heaving, sweat puddling around her, and every muscle barking at her to quit.

At school, she thought she was in shape. In fact, she made it a point to wake up well before her classes and run almost every day. But, as is becoming quickly obvious, jogging at a leisurely pace for a few miles is no way to prepare for the punishment she's now enduring.

Hovering over her as she tries to catch her breath is a short, muscular, dark haired trainer named Isaac. He's holding a 10-pound weight in each hand and waiting impatiently for Shira to recover enough so he can torture her again. The weights are so light in his hands that he juggles them as he peers at her, both hurrying and insulting her, at the same time.

When Shira finally decides she's ready, the trainer gives her the weights and has her hold them while she does short, fast bursts of running, forward, backward, and sideways. The goal is to improve her reaction time, a critical skill for field agents.

Then, to test her further, he puts her through an obstacle course, simulating a variety of real life situations.

Cardboard cutouts of fake gunmen pop out suddenly in front of her and dummies are thrown at her as she tries to get from one end of the gymnasium to the other, all the time carrying the 10-pound weights.

When Shira is totally exhausted and no longer able to do what the trainer wants, he leads her down the hall to a small unmarked room.

Once inside, she finds, well, almost nothing. No windows. No paint or art on the walls. Only a cheap wooden table in the center of the room, with a straight backed chair tucked under it. If the goal of her handlers is to add to her discomfort, this room is perfect.

On the table sits an antique lamp surrounded by piles of old dog eared books and scraps of paper. Everything smells musty, and except for the small halo of light from a single lamp, the room is dark and foreboding.

Each book has multi-colored bookmarks stuck in its pages, obviously meant to guide Shira to the sections her handlers want her to learn. They include such things as Israeli history, past Mossad operations, and the doctrines of various Arab groups.

Shira begins her studying. She learns not only who the leaders of dozens of Arab states are, but also, what personal weaknesses they have and how best to exploit them if necessary. She works on various Arabic languages and dialects, all of which come easily to her, and the long, brutal, histories, of Arab-Israeli conflicts, which do not.

As she reads, Shira is mildly surprised at the brutal honesty of the materials selected. Dozens of Arab atrocities are covered vividly, of course, but so are Jewish ones. And, if there is a political slant, it leans toward the Muslim side. Her handlers must believe Shira is already sufficiently versed in Israeli doctrine, and they don't want to waste time convincing her of things she already believes.

Instead, they want Shira to understand, and appreciate, the Arab point of view. They obviously believe that the more she internalizes their customs and belief systems, the more instinctual her reactions will be in the field.

Shira reads highlighted sections of the Koran and even memorizes some verses and chapters that may be useful to quote later. She knows that she will be put in situations where not only her knowledge but her heart will be tested, and to be ready, she needs to think like an Arab, not a Jew.

Still, it doesn't take much reading to realize that all Arab societies, no matter how moderate they seem, are incredibly patriarchal. Shira will be entering a very unfamiliar world where women are, at best, second-class citizens.

Still, she knows that, if she's to portray a Muslim woman, she has to be authentically subservient; something that, for her, will be much harder than remembering Arab customs, or speaking their language.

How to wear a Burka? That's the easy part.

How to avert her eyes, shrink from confrontation, and refrain from speaking her mind, those things will be much harder.

****

Just when Shira is at her wit's end, when each day is way too crowded with physical and mental training, and when she is feeling more alone than at any other time in her life, there is a welcome respite.

Out of the blue, Aaron Schwartz calls her at home and asks to meet her for coffee.

"Aaron, what a sight for sore eyes," she says as she approaches him at a back table in a small cafe near the training facility. "What in the world are you doing here in Tel Aviv?"

They embrace and Shira sits down, still holding both of his hands.

"I'm here all of the time now," he finally replies. "I would have called earlier, but I didn't know you were in Tel Aviv until a few days ago. After you left medical school I kind of lost track of you and if you hadn't told your roommate your phone number, I would have lost you forever."

"Don't be so melodramatic," Shira says. "I knew how to get in touch with you."

"Ah, but would you?" Aaron asks. "That's the question."

"Of course, I would," she answers, "when the time was right."

"So, what are you doing in Tel Aviv?" He asks, obviously still curious about what made her quit medicine.

"More schooling," Shira answers quickly. "And what are you doing here?"

"I'm still on the same mission, you know, trying to solve the Mideast problem, all by myself. One step forward, two back. I manage Arab-Israeli symposiums here, and in Jerusalem as well, and even in Palestine on occasion."

"To do what exactly?"

"We get political, business, and religious leaders together, both Jewish and Muslim, to discuss our differences. And we hope that, as we talk, our similarities will emerge," Aaron explains, "and we can find common ground."

"Do you?" Shira asks, determined to keep the conversation focused on what Aaron is doing, and away from her.

"Not as often as I would like," he answers. "It's amazing how much our day-to-day lives, whether Israeli or Arab, are infected by the hatred and revenge of our forefathers. You've probably already seen that first-hand."

"What do you mean?"

"I'm sure that Muslim doctors can be impressed by the skill of Jewish doctors but, still, have no respect for them as people. Anyway, I'm not very optimistic. But you got me off the subject. I'm curious. What exactly are you doing now? When you say more schooling, what do you mean by that?"

"You know, maybe a Master's degree or something," Shira responds. "I'm just not ready for the real world yet."

When Aaron starts to ask another question, Shira shushes him by saying, "Why don't we continue this conversation in your hotel room."

Not surprisingly, when alone in his room, they don't continue it. In fact, by the time their love-making is over, Aaron has lost all interest in her schooling. Or anything else, for that matter. In fact, within five minutes, he's fast asleep.

And, the next morning, when he wakes up, she's long gone.

****

"I don't care how discrete you were, you have to get rid of him," Ari says, emphatically.

Shira has finally worked up the courage to tell her boss about the re-kindled romance she's enjoying with Aaron. Keeping her job a secret from her "boyfriend" has become untenable and Shira feels that, given an appropriate explanation, Ari will undoubtedly relent.

It turns out she's wrong.

"But I love him," Shira blurts out, thinking how strange it is that her first time saying those words was not to Aaron, but to this little gnome of a man who has the gall to tell her who she can and cannot date.

"Doesn't matter," Ari replies. "We can't have any romantic complications at this point in your training. If you aren't willing to give him up, we'll shake hands and part friends. No hard feelings."

After such an ultimatum, she thinks, *I doubt we'll be parting friends, Mr. Spymaster.*

"But surely you can't expect me to be celibate, like a nun," Shira counters.

"I didn't say that. I just don't want you to get so close to a man that we are forced to have this conversation again."

"Ever again?"

"Or at least until you've proven yourself," Ari corrects himself.

"Sounds like you're advocating a pretty loose lifestyle," Shira counters.

"Look," he replies. "For the time being, you have to decide between this young man and your career. It happens all the time. Let me know your decision."

And, he looks back down at the papers on his desk, effectively dismissing her.

But Shira doesn't move. She's furious.

Finally, Ari looks up again, a more sympathetic look on his face.

"I know how hard it is for you, Shira," he says, "how alone you must feel at times. Normally, a young girl like you would confide in her parents, get support from them, and I would be all right with that. But, given that you're estranged from them, that isn't really an alternative, is it?"

"No, it isn't."

"Also, I wish we had more female agents around so you could network with them," Ari goes on. "But, shame on us, we don't. Hopefully that will change going forward."

"I knew that I would have to prove myself, Ari," Shira responds. "I didn't expect a brass band. But I thought you would be more flexible, and the other agents more accepting. It's not as if they're giving me the cold shoulder. They're not giving me anything at all. It's as if they don't expect me to be around very long."

"Honestly, they don't. So far, our track record with female agents hasn't been very good."

"But they should give me a chance to prove myself, one way or the other."

"You would think that, wouldn't you," he agrees, sounding a little more sympathetic, "but our agents aren't like most people. They're not exactly warm and fuzzy. And, they're highly competitive. Pretty black and white thinkers. Then, when you add in their natural distrust of somebody new, especially a female agent with no experience, it can become a difficult situation."

"Difficult situation, Ari? That's a bit of an understatement, don't you think?"

"Yes, but not impossible."

"Believe me, I'm not throwing in the towel yet. Still, I'm not a very social person. As you probably already know. It takes a while for me to trust people. And, I finally had a soulmate in Aaron."

"Look, Shira, your relationship with Aaron is non-negotiable. We can't have you talking to any boyfriends, no matter how close they may be to you" he reiterates. "Is that understood?"

"Yes, sir," Shira answers reluctantly.

"But I have a thought," he goes on. "My secretary, Eliana, knows more about what goes on in this agency than I do. She's a very nice person, who can provide you a sympathetic ear now and again. And I trust her implicitly. Why don't you spend some time with her? Especially when you're feeling down. I think she can help you put things into perspective."

"I don't need a baby sitter."

"That's not what I'm suggesting," Ari counters. "In fact, I'll let her know that anything you tell her is confidential. She's to tell no one."

"Not even you."

"Especially me."

"OK. I'll talk to her," Shira concedes. "Although I doubt that'll help much."

"And you need to talk to Aaron as well," Ari circles back to the original point. "He has to go. Is that clear?"

Shira stares into Ari's eyes, sees no equivocation, and finally relents.

"Yes, boss. No Aaron. I'll keep him at arms-length. At least for now."

Ari is quiet for a few seconds. He's obviously weighing whether he can trust Shira. Finally, he says, "OK, Shira, I'll take you at your word."

And he is right to do that.

Because, upon reflection, Shira realizes that being a Mossad agent is something she isn't about to give up on just yet. No boyfriend is worth that at this point. Not even Aaron.

****

It turns out that Ari's instinct is spot on as regards Eliana Baum. She's exactly the person Shira needs as a confidante, not only to keep her spirits up, but to answer questions about the agency that Ari wouldn't, or couldn't.

Eliana is in her forties, not old by any stretch of the imagination, but she acts older and way more mature than Shira, or most of the other agents at headquarters.

Even better, she has a presence that transcends her position. People gravitate toward Eliana, not just because she has Ari's ear, but also because she shares his knowledge and common sense. When Eliana "guesses" what Ari thinks, you can pretty much take it to the bank.

But you wouldn't know how influential she is just by looking at her. Her dull, brown hair is tied back in a bun, off her face, with streaks of gray peppering it, not as a hairdresser might do it, but as Mother Nature does. Her face is pleasant and expressive. Clear, scrubbed skin. No makeup. A hint of dimples on either side of an aesthetically pleasing Greek nose.

But the piece de resistance is her mouth, which can turn upward in a radiant smile or downward in a frown, depending on the circumstances, making her entire face highly expressive.

And, not surprisingly, Eliana dresses conservatively, in long dresses and blazers, completing a business-like look that fits her position perfectly.

Shira was a little hesitant to approach Eliana directly but she needn't have been. As in keeping with her position and personality, Eliana made the first move.

"Shira, how about we have coffee tomorrow," she asked. "Say 10 a.m. in the cafeteria?"

The next morning when Shira arrives to the cafeteria ten minutes early, as is her custom, she's surprised to find Eliana already there, a big friendly smile on her face, motioning to the chair across from her.

"Have a seat, Shira," she says. "I've taken the liberty of ordering a pot for us to share. Do you take your coffee black? Or with cream or sugar?"

"Black is great."

Eliana pours Shira a cup, and hesitates a minute before opening the conversation.

"So, let me say how honored I am to be formally meeting with you. In the few months you've been around here you've already become pretty famous. You breezed through training easier than any agent before you, male or female."

"Really?" Shira asks. "It doesn't feel like I've been breezing through anything. And Ari certainly hasn't said that."

"If you want a compliment out of that man, believe me, you'll be sorely disappointed," Eliana replies. "He's got a good mind, and a good heart, but his people skills could use some work. I don't know why he isn't more open with people. Maybe he was born that way but, more likely, it's a learned behavior, molded by his experiences here."

"I suppose he's been in quite a few harrowing situations."

"You have no idea," Eliana says. "Like you, he was a young protege at one time. Part of a brave and heroic group of men who changed the world. Well, at least our world. We owe him a lot."

"Are his buddies at the agency still around?"

"That's the thing. No, they aren't. And, given his position here, I don't think he'll have buddies like that ever again."

"Pretty sad."

"He's reconciled to it," Eliana responds. "No buddies probably. But favorites. And believe me, right now, you're one of those. He'll do anything to have you succeed."

"Lots of pressure," Shira confides.

"I wouldn't look at it that way," Eliana responds. "You're young. You're idealistic. You have a long life ahead of you. Don't shorten it by worrying about things you can't do anything about. Just give each assignment your best shot, and I'm sure that'll be good enough."

"At times, I'm not so sure of that."

"Of course, you're not sure. But that's the fun of it, isn't it? You didn't join the Mossad to be sure of what's ahead. You wanted the excitement of not knowing. Right?"

"I guess."

"Shira, you're in a position many of us would kill to be in," Eliana says. "You're going to have experiences very few people get to have. And, as a bonus, you can make a real difference for Israel, and the Jewish people everywhere."

"That's why I'm here," Shira responds. "But I don't want to miss out on my youth in the process."

"What do you mean?"

"Ari told me I have to give up my boyfriend. That's a pretty big price to pay."

"You mean Aaron Schwartz?"

"How did you know his name?" Shira asks.

"You would be surprised what the agency knows," Eliana answers. "And, if the agency knows it, I know it."

Shira is a bit taken aback. Not by Eliana's bragging about her agency knowledge, of course. Ari had hinted as much. But by the fact that the agency cared about Shira's boyfriends enough to have a dossier on Aaron.

"So, the agency is keeping tabs on my boyfriends?"

"Not all of them," Eliana replies. "Just him. From what I understand he has close relationships with a number of powerful Arabs."

"That's his job. He tries to bring difference-makers together, both Jewish and Muslim."

"Well," Eliana clarifies. "From what I understand, his relationships have raised some flags. Not enough to arrest

48

him or anything. But, certainly, enough to keep you from cavorting with him."

"Eliana, if it helps, I can assure you that I haven't told Aaron anything. He doesn't even know where I work."

"I suspect he's figured that out," Eliana replies. "But you don't have to tell me anything. I'm a nobody. In fact, I would get in trouble if Ari knew I told you this much. I just felt you had a right to know."

"Of course, I have a right to know," Shira shouts. "And Ari should have told me."

"I'm sure he has his reasons, but please don't tell him what I said. I'm way out on a limb here."

"Of course, I won't. And thank you, Eliana. Your friendship is important to me. I really need somebody to talk to."

"Well, Shira, while I'm blabbing, you should know that Ari plans to step up your training with an assignment outside Israel."

"Really? Where?"

"Ever been to Paris?" Eliana says with a wink.

Chapter 4
Paris

Paul Mersault is a good-looking Frenchman who, with his equally attractive wife, Sofia, could be modeling for high-end fashion magazines.

But instead, they are wealthy, young socialites who arrived in town just a few weeks ago, and with no formal introductions, exploded prominently onto the Paris party scene.

There was a time when such a thing would have been impossible. You needed credentials and impeccable references to get invitations. But now, one only has to have the wit and style to make any party better. Which is why the Mersaults have been so quickly accepted.

Virtually nothing is known about them. Word has it that Paul inherited his wealth from his aunt, but nobody knows who she was, or where she got her money, or even how he got his hands on it.

And Sofia is thought to be a physician by training, but given her active nightlife, it's unlikely that she's actually practicing. No doctor could burn the candle at both ends the way this couple is.

It's also rumored that the two of them grew up in the north of France. Rouen, perhaps. Or Normandy. But their social skills suggest they've traveled extensively since then.

At the Paris events they've attended, Paul's engaging stories, and Sofia's flirtatious manner have made them very popular, a sort of flame around which the jeweled and jaded socialite moths of Paris are currently flitting.

And, among the moths drawn to the Mersaults is the mysterious Muslim monarch, Sheik Mohammed Khalil.

Just forty-five years-old and extremely rich, the Sheik from Saudi Arabia makes it a habit to plug into the Parisian night life every so often just to see what, and who, is fresh and new.

Given his omniscient presence at openings, shows, and other events, Mohammed might be mistaken for a social climber, except for the fact that he's already reached the top rung of his social hierarchy. He has status, power, and money.

So, what the Sheik is after now is not that unusual for somebody who has everything else. His primary goal in mid-life is to attract, catch, and collect as many beautiful women as possible. Women like Sofia.

Surprisingly, Paul seems oblivious to the rather heavy handed way Sheik Mohammed has been pursuing his wife. Perhaps Paul doesn't care or, more likely, he's just gotten used to it over the years. He must know from experience that, by evening's end, Mohammed, or any other Sofia suitors for that matter, will go home disappointed, and empty handed.

But actually, there's another reason Paul isn't worried about somebody stealing his wife. That's because, well, she isn't really his wife at all. In fact, he hardly knows her. She's just been assigned to assist him on this operation.

In truth, Sofia, is actually Shira on her maiden voyage as a Mossad operative. She's under the watchful eye of Ari, who is undercover as well, as he plays the role of an inconspicuous, dumpy-looking, little man lurking at the back of the ballroom. Not much of a stretch.

Ari is pleased. Shira is proving to be exactly what he had hoped for when he recruited her, a born actress who can slip into any role as easily as she slipped into the silk dress she's just barely wearing at the moment.

Still, her act has not been perfect. For one thing, Shira has been too playful with Mohammed, which, although normally one of her strong suits, really isn't such a good idea with him.

Ari makes a mental note to tell Shira she should be less aggressive. Pursuing Muslim men without offending them can be tricky and dangerous. It's better to let them pursue you. And Shira has what it takes to make that happen.

But, of course, Shira doesn't know that yet. She hasn't interacted much with older, more sophisticated men, certainly not Muslim men, which is why Ari set up this training operation in the first place. Just one more thing for Shira to learn on a path toward becoming one of Ari's most important assets, which he's now certain will happen sooner rather than later.

****

Sheik Mohammed Khalil is in love, perhaps for the first time in his life.

His courtship of Sofia Mersault (aka Shira) hasn't been all smooth sailing, that's for sure. She seemed shocked, even insulted, when, shortly after they first met, the Sheik called to ask her out to lunch.

As any happily married woman would do, Sofia declined quickly, and hung up. Subsequent calls went unanswered, signaling her lack of interest.

A less ardent pursuer might have given up but Mohammed had not only the desire but also the means, to keep after her. He even hired a detective to monitor the couple's activities and once he knew exactly when Paul would be gone, he had flowers and elaborate presents delivered at those exact times.

Sofia could have refused his gifts but she didn't, and the Sheik was encouraged. There was light at the end at the end of his passion fueled tunnel. Eventually, Mohammed had his chauffeur show up at Sofia's door with an engraved invitation to join him at a concert that very night.

The uniformed man waited outside the front door while Sofia dressed in a gown hand-selected by Ari for just such an occasion. The old Mossad handler had chosen well, and when Sofia slid into her seat at the opera house, she attracted every eye in the house, both male and female. The Sheik could not have been more pleased.

Now, several weeks into the affair, Ari is ready to initiate the second phase of his training exercise for Shira in her role as Sofia.

By design, every attempt Mohammed has made to escalate the romance beyond kissing and hand-holding has been rebuffed. But Ari knows the clock is ticking. So, it's time to see if his young agent can deliver something of value for their efforts.

It turns out that the Sheik is not just a pampered philanderer. On behalf of the Saudi government, he has been intimately involved with the latest negotiations to sell oil to the United States, and the Mossad spymaster happens to know that right now, in his briefcase, is a summary of offers that will be presented at a conference in Helsinki the following week. The U.S will pay dearly for that information and although this is primarily a training exercise, Ari thinks, *Why not steal something valuable in the process?*

"Mohammed, darling," Sofia asks. "Would you mind fetching my jacket? I'm a little chilled."

It's 1:00 p.m. and they're having lunch in the bar of the Savoy Hotel, where the Sheik is staying before flying into Helsinki the next day.

Since Paul is conveniently out of town, Sofia has agreed to sleep with Mohammed for the first time that afternoon, and so, after drinking a bottle of champagne that has fueled his ardor, he is being uncharacteristically accommodating.

"Here," Mohammed offers, shedding his suit coat. "Take my jacket. I don't need it."

He's uncomfortable leaving his prize catch unattended, and also worries about the briefcase stowed under his chair.

But Sofia is insistent.

"I wouldn't think of taking your coat from you. Please, our lunch won't be here for some time. I really would like my own."

She looks so innocent, so helpless, so infatuated, how can he refuse her?

So, the Sheik looks around for somebody to help but finds himself remarkably unattended. He then remembers that, because he was planning to consummate his lengthy courtship this very afternoon, he had let his chauffeur and attendant take the rest of the day off. His thinking was that what he intended to do for the rest of the afternoon and evening was best done alone. Well, not entirely alone, of course. He hoped to have a willing partner in Sofia.

So, without servants, and not willing to risk upsetting his beautiful prey at this point in the hunt, Mohammed does something wholly uncharacteristic of Arab royalty. He decides to retrieve her coat himself.

Rising unsteadily, he starts to reach for the briefcase but thinks better of it. At best, carrying it with him would look like he doesn't trust her and at worst, she might think that he's not coming back at all. So, he leaves it.

Big mistake.

Seconds after Mohammed's departure, two unfamiliar men pass by the table, nod at Shira, and take the briefcase.

Nobody briefed her on what would happen once the Sheik left, so she's surprised at the clumsiness of the intercept. She had expected something much more sophisticated. Why two men, for instance? And what if other diners saw them?

But what concerns Shira the most is that she has no idea what is supposed to happen next. Will the briefcase be returned before the Sheik gets back? And, if he suspects something, and asks questions, how should she respond? Probably just smile and look pretty. And then improvise. Not exactly her strong suit.

Across the room, Shira sees the hotel elevator door open and there is Mohammed, carrying her coat over his arm and walking briskly toward her. Unfortunately, his briefcase has not been returned.

She's only seconds away from disaster when suddenly, out of nowhere, a waiter enters stage right, carrying a tray of drinks. He tries to avoid the Sheik, but both are moving too fast and, as they collide, the tray slithers out of the waiter's grasp, sending drinks in all directions.

Both men are apologetic, of course, but the damage is done. Diners leave their tables, not sure what they can do, but certainly willing to help. Other waiters hurry over, with mops and brooms to clean up the mess. They motion people away, worried that the glass will cut somebody. And for a second, there's utter chaos.

Of course, nobody is watching Shira's table and she's surprised that, once the commotion has died down, there is the briefcase, sitting beside the Sheik's chair, as if it had been there all along.

Also, in front of her is a folded note that reads, "Extricate yourself as quickly as possible."

That is so Mossad, she thinks. Impersonal. Abrupt. And very clear.

When Mohammed finally arrives at the table, Sofia kisses him on the cheek, then excuses herself to go to the powder room. Only she doesn't do that, of course. She goes directly out the front doors, leaving the hotel, and the Sheik, forever.

Mohammed will never see her again because Sofia will never exist again. Training exercise over.

****

The next day, however, Shira walks right past Eliana and barges into Ari's office unannounced, yelling at him loudly enough for his secretary to hear, "That was fucking amateur hour, Ari."

He just smiles back.

Ari is in a particularly good mood because he knows something the rest of the team will never know, that the information they got from Mohammed was incredibly valuable to the United States, and the operation was a huge success.

The Prime Minister is happy. The Director of Mossad is happy. And Ari Lavon is really happy. It seems the only one not happy at the moment is Shira, who is angry enough to crawl over his desk and assault him.

"You put me in an impossible situation," she shouts rather impertinently. "I had no idea what to expect. Because of your incredible lack of planning, my cover could have been blown. And I could have been in danger."

"But it wasn't. And you weren't."

"Doesn't matter. I demand to be in on everything from the beginning next time," Shira continues her rant.

"OK," Ari whispers.

"And I won't take no for an answer."

Shira either hasn't heard him or she's just going through the script as she's been practicing it.

"OK," Ari says a little louder.

"What?"

"OK. You're right. From now on, I will include you in the planning," Ari says, still smiling.

And, now, everybody is happy. Even Eliana, who enjoyed the show immensely.

Chapter 5
Beirut

Given her success in Paris, Shira has been given a new, more important, training assignment. She's going to Beirut, Lebanon pretending to be Peggy Jenkins, a student from Cleveland, Ohio who's working on a doctorate degree in biology at the American University.

She's being placed in the home of a mid-level government official, and although her primary goal is to gather any intel from him that will help Israel approach the new administration, her secondary goal is to socialize with the family, and gauge the heart and will of the Lebanese people, something that might matter more than what a mid-level government official does.

Ari characterizes Shira's assignment as intelligence gathering only, meaning that there is no single well-defined objective or time frame. Shira will plan on the fly, improvise as necessary, and do whatever it takes to gather information that can help her government.

It's a major step-up in Shira's training, kind of like a neophyte pilot taking her first solo flight, and it certainly affirms how highly Ari, and the Mossad, judge her performance to date. She will nominally report to Ari but, since he will be in Tel Aviv, the vast majority of day-to-day decision making will fall on her shoulders, and hers alone.

Ari has chosen the family for Shira carefully, not only because of the father's job but, also, because the family has rented rooms to students from the U.S. before and the whole family speaks passable English.

The head of the family is Majed Kahn. His wife is Zaina and they have one daughter, Raya. The family's ad said that they preferred somebody who could help their daughter with her English, no stretch for Shira and a win-win for the Kahns. Sort of like getting an older sister for their daughter and a tutor as well, all while collecting rent.

Shira will pretend to be several years younger than she actually is, and a little nerdier as well. So, in contrast to her last role as Sofia, she will have to downplay her looks, with no makeup, glasses and ill-fitting clothes.

Ari does a good job of selling Peggy to the Kahns, and her written application is accepted quickly. But, the final step, an interview with the family, promises to be more challenging, and Majed himself is there to do the questioning.

He's a stern, taciturn man with a Stalin-like mustache that makes him look older than his forty-two years. Still, his eyes are young and twinkling, belying the image he's trying to project in his clothes and manner.

"How do you feel about Muslims?" he asks after reviewing Shira's carefully crafted resume.

"Well, I'm a Christian. But I guess Muslims are all right," Shira answers like an American teenager might.

"All right?" Majed says, a bit derisively. "You have a lot to learn."

"That's why I'm here."

"Really? I wondered about that. Why would an American come here, now, in the midst of a civil war?"

"American University has an excellent reputation in my field," Shira answers. "I hope to be a college professor and they have a great record of getting jobs for people like me."

"But Lebanon? Now? Really?"

"I plan to teach in Beirut. Or somewhere around here. And, honestly, do you really think I can escape civil wars anywhere in the Middle East right now?" She counters. "Besides, I'm told it's relatively safe for Americans."

"It's not safe for anybody," Majed counters authoritatively.

"I'll be careful," Shira replies.

"Not possible."

"If it's so risky, why are you here, Mr. Kahn?"

"It's my country, my duty, Miss Jenkins," Majed says, sitting up more erect in his chair. "I have a job to do, and if it comes with some risk, I'm willing to accept that."

Shira goes for the jugular. "And your wife? Your daughter? Are they willing to take the risk?"

Majed looks over at the two women he loves more than life itself. Both are wearing hijabs. Their faces are uncovered, their heads are tilted, and eyes down. They say nothing, but seem to be listening intently.

The American girl's point is well-taken, Majed thinks. *Who is he to question her decision, made of her own free will, when he's made the same decision for his own family?*

He stares at Shira for a few more seconds, making her shift uneasily in her chair. Finally, he thinks, *this young girl is astute, and strong willed. Maybe having her live with us will provide a good role model for my daughter.*

"OK. The room is yours," he says, never suspicioning that he has just let a newly minted Israeli spy into the inner sanctum of his home, his family, and his life.

In just a few weeks, Shira has integrated into the Kahn family more seamlessly than could be expected. She even joins the family occasionally on their morning walks around the neighborhood, a gated community like those found in the suburbs of most major cities.

Only, here, the guard is heavily armed.

When Shira eats with the family, they occasionally speak English, and Shira is encouraged to join in. Most of the time, however, they speak their own language, not knowing, of course, that, given her studies, Shira can piece together a little bit of what they're saying. Still, she doesn't learn much of value.

Although Majed likes to talk about things that happen at work, who's up for promotion, who's having a baby, and the like; he's tight-lipped about the things that interest Shira the most, like geopolitical strategies, economic policies, and especially the government's view of Israel.

Fortunately, Raja has taken a liking to Peggy and she includes the American in many of her social activities with friends, where Shira learns much more than she does from dinner conversations with Majed.

So, ironically, much of what's in Shira's initial reports comes not from confidential government sources, as originally intended, but from open and candid discussions between teenage girls and their families, the same sort of gossip that back home might be deemed frivolous.

Yet, it is proving more valuable to the Mossad than what they have been getting through their own, more official, channels. Surprisingly, Shira is turning out to be a talented reporter, and an important source of intel.

Of course, much of the appeal of her reports is because of the story line, which is fast-moving and eventful. Like a compelling novel, there are continuous twists and never-ending dramas in the Lebanese government that capture the attention of everybody on her distribution list.

Not only is there a civil war raging between Christians and Muslims, but the Lebanese government is in complete disarray as they try to transition to new leadership amid the chaos.

Nobody living in Beirut knows what's really happening, even those in the government, and their shared discomfort is palpable. There's a desperate thirst for knowledge that, with communication lines as broken down as they are, is hard to sate. Bombs are scary. But fear of the unknown even more so.

Shira's writing about these events is timely, succinct, and occasionally actionable, which is surprising given how raw and untrained she is.

In fact, in terms of providing context, her reports have quickly become required reading at the highest levels of the Mossad, and occasionally, even higher.

But, it's probably due more to the pace of events in Lebanon than her writing skills. Just days before Shira moved in with the Khans, the National Assembly of Lebanon elected Elias Sarkis its president in a hotly contested election that did little to calm the waters politically. In fact, in protest, twenty-nine members of the Assembly boycotted the session, and the previous president refused to leave office.

So, Sarkis, the new president, had to be sworn in at a hotel 25 miles outside Beirut and wasn't able to officially assume office right away, leaving Majed, and his fellow government workers, demotivated and leaderless.

Although he tries not to say much in front of Shira, the frustration Majed is feeling about the situation is evident in the Khan household. Everybody is on pins and needles, worrying about Majed, of course, but also about the future of their country.

Shira chronicles everything as best she can in an attempt to give her bosses a sense of what is happening, not only behind closed government doors, which is very little, but, also, in the homes and streets of the troubled city.

Shira spends many of her days out and around, talking to anybody she can. On one hand, people are skeptical of someone so obviously non-Lebanese asking questions. But, on the other hand, they wonder whether she knows something they don't. So, they engage with her.

Eventually, because of what Shira learns and reports, the government of Israel decides to wait a few weeks before officially contacting the new Lebanese government. Their hope is that the roles and power structure will be more firmly established by then.

It turns out to be a wise decision, and Shira's stock rises even further.

In the meantime, the current Prime Minister of Lebanon, Rashid Karami is forced to make some very important decisions on his own, all of which Shira outlines in her reports. Among them is his refusal to allow French peacekeeping forces into the country, a decision heavily debated in homes, nightclubs, and cafes all over Beirut, and not fully understood by the Kahn's friends.

The line between friends and enemies of Lebanon is becoming increasingly blurred, and dependent not so much on who the government supports but on who the various sects within Lebanon support.

The government is becoming increasingly irrelevant, which can't be a good thing for Lebanon long-term. Understandably, the Kahn family, and their friends, are despondent and depressed about the future. All of this Shira lays out in her reports.

Then, a few days later, when 12,000 Syrian troops intervene in support of the Lebanese government, these same people flip emotionally, and celebrate, feeling that the scales have tipped toward some form of ceasefire. Maybe even peace. Which, to them, is the over-riding objective right now. Shira dutifully reports that as well.

It's near the end of June and everything is going well for her. She's fully embedded. The Khan family trusts her, and Majed has even hinted at bringing her into his offices to meet colleagues, perhaps the beginning of a relationship that could result in better informed intel beneficial to Israel.

So, it's a huge shock to Shira when, on the afternoon of June 27, with no explanation or warning, she's ordered to return to Tel Aviv immediately.

Chapter 6
Tel Aviv

Shira has been waiting outside Ari's office, talking to his secretary for a while now. But surprisingly, Eliana says she knows nothing about why Shira was recalled from Beirut.

It's unusual for Ari to make me wait, she mutters to herself. *I expected him to bolt out of the office, greet me warmly, and ask about my experiences in Beirut.*

But, so far, Shira has been left alone to ponder what Ari has in store for her now. It must be pretty big, she thinks, to drag her away from what she had been told was a highly successful operation.

Ari's door is closed but, still, she can hear multiple voices rising and falling in a way that hints at frayed nerves and raw emotions. She even hears somebody slam the desk with their hand. Big or not, whatever is being discussed sounds serious. There's no laughter, unusual for agency meetings like this, since the kind of work they do is a breeding ground for a unique brand of dark humor.

Shira just hopes that whatever they're discussing doesn't involve her. But, given the fact that she's been called back to Tel Aviv and asked to sit outside Ari's office while this meeting is going on, how can it not?

Finally, the door opens and three stony-faced men pass by her with no acknowledgement. None are familiar, but that's hardly unusual given that she went straight from her training to Paris and then, Beirut. There wasn't really any time for Shira to get to know anybody at headquarters, especially those in authority.

Shira waits impatiently for Ari to invite her in but, surprisingly, he doesn't. So, eventually she peeks through the open door at the little, but powerful man who recruited her. He's slumped over his desk, face buried in his hands, a sight that Shira never thought she'd see.

What in the world, she thinks, could cause one of the most strong-willed men she's ever met to appear so weak, and pitiful.

Finally, he looks up, sees her in the doorway and with the wave of his hand, invites her to join him. She sits down in the chair directly across from him and waits while he shuffles some papers, obviously trying to compose himself a little before addressing her.

Shira's anger has dissipated, replaced by curiosity, and concern. She holds her tongue, and her questions, until Ari sits up in his chair, stares at the ceiling for a few minutes, then, finally, looks directly into her eyes, and begins to speak.

"We have a situation," he begins. "A bad situation. It started yesterday with the hijacking of an Air France flight from Tel Aviv to Paris through Athens."

"Yes, I heard something about that. But how does it involve us?" Shira replies.

"Everything involves us, Shira. You should know that by now."

Ari is testier than normal and Shira decides to shut up and listen for a change. What she's really thinking, however, is more self-oriented.

How might the hijacking of an airplane going to Paris involve her? Why would Ari pull her away from one of the hottest spots in the Middle East? And to do what exactly?

"I'll be brief," Ari finally says. "Yesterday some Germans boarded an Air France plane in Athens and took the cockpit by force. After the release of fifty-three of the passengers, they demanded five million dollars for the rest. When that request was refused, the plane was flown to Benghazi, then to Entebbe airport in Uganda, which is where the hostages are now. They have two-hundred forty-eight passengers and twelve crew members still on board," Ari continues, "many of them Israelis."

Shira's eyebrows arch, but she says nothing. The picture is getting clearer.

"We don't trust the President of Uganda, a guy named Idi Amin. It appears he won't help us at all, so any rescue attempt will have to be done by the Israeli military alone."

Shira knows that the army has units of highly-trained professionals on standby, ready for a situation like this. Well, maybe not exactly like this. Not as complicated or public perhaps. But it isn't unheard of for Israel to try to extract hostages by force using soldiers specially trained for that kind of operation. What's unheard of, she thinks, is to involve an inexperienced agent like her.

"We have Israeli officials in Uganda who are providing information as best they can," Ari goes on. "But they aren't intelligence specialists."

"Neither am I," Shira interrupts for the first time.

She's worried about where this is going and wants to head it off as quickly as possible. She wants nothing to do with a military raid. And, strangely, she longs for the relative safety of her newly-adopted home in Beirut.

"I know that, and we have experienced people already on their way to Uganda," Ari says, "but it has been suggested that you can be useful in a way perhaps none of our other operatives can. You obviously have a unique ability to gather information and report on it."

"I'm an operative now?" Shira asks.

"Let's call it a 'battlefield promotion'. Of course, you could go back to being a 'trainee' again, or even lower, in a heartbeat," Ari says in a tone that shows he's regaining his sense of humor.

"Way to motivate me," Shira responds. "OK. What's the assignment?"

"I want you to fly into Uganda tonight," Ari continues. "And, like in Beirut, your objective is to help us understand the situation on the ground, as best you can. And to figure out alternatives for entering and exiting the terminal, in case we have to do something militarily."

Shira starts to object but Ari shushes her.

"You really have no choice in the matter. This plan has been approved by the highest levels of our government," he says. "And, as soon as we're done here, you'll be given a briefing by people much more capable than me."

"Nobody is more capable than—" Shira starts to say but Ari shushes her.

"Unfortunately, in this case, you may be right," Ari agrees. "I don't think that they know much more than I do. So, hopefully, you can fill in the blanks when you get there."

"Will I be given access to the airport terminal?" Shira asks. "I can't really help if I can't see the situation up close."

"Good question. Here's where it gets kind of tricky," Ari explains. "We've arranged for selected relatives of hostages and crew members to be sequestered in another section of the terminal building, near the hostages. Our cover story is that we want to comfort anybody who's released, and do it quickly. Call it PR or whatever. You're going to be in that small group."

"In what capacity?" Shira is skeptical.

"The pilot of the plane, Michel Bacos, is a married Frenchman and you're going to be his wife."

"Really? Will that work? How old is she?"

"In her forties I think, but, with a bit of makeup, we believe you can pass. There's a resemblance already. In fact, that's what triggered the idea in the first place."

"Was this your idea?" Shira asks.

"Higher. Much higher," Ari answers. "Your papers are being prepared as we speak and they will be given to you right after you land at Entebbe. We don't think anybody will be checking them closely anyway, if at all. But we want you to be covered just in case."

"What if they release the pilot before I get there or, even worse, while I'm there?" Shira asks.

"We have it on good authority that Mr. Bacos will remain with the hostages no matter what," Ari answers. "He sees himself as responsible somehow. And insists that he be the last one released."

"What a guy, my husband. But, if he is released into my arms, say, what then?"

"Well, I hear he's a pretty good-looking guy. So how bad can it be?" Ari quips.

"Seriously. What do I do then?"

"Wing it, Shira. As always, wing it."

As Shira leaves Ari's office, Eliana asks her what's up.

"You'll have to talk to your boss about that, I'm afraid," Shira answers. "I'm not sure what I can or can't tell you at this point. But it's something big."

"Fair enough," Eliana answers, "but Ari asked me to check in with you on the situation in Beirut. I've read your reports. But I'm curious. Are you getting along OK with the Kahn's? Do they suspect anything? And how are you feeling about things at this point?"

Shira looks around to see if they're alone. Then she whispers, "Actually, Eliana, I would love to talk to you about Beirut. Or anything else for that matter, except my new confidential assignment. Are you free for coffee?"

A few minutes later, when the two women are comfortably seated at a back table in the cafeteria, far from prying eyes and ears, Shira really opens up.

"It is so lonely there," she says. "I had no idea how hard it would be to stay in character all of the time, with no one to share thoughts and experiences with. Every minute is nerve-wracking, and scary."

"What do you mean?"

"Well, the simplest of questions," Shira explains. "Like, have you ever been to California? Are the beaches as great as people say they are? And Hollywood? What's that like? Who are your favorite movie stars? All of the ordinary questions you might expect from a teen age daughter. All of them require ad-libbing on my part, and then, I have to remember what I ad-libbed. There's no such thing as a casual conversation."

"Sounds intense," Eliana agrees.

"It is, but what's worse is that there's no let-up," Shira goes on. "You're playing a role in a play that never ends. And, instead of a bad review, you could end up dead."

"Those of us here back here can't really appreciate what you're going through."

"Frankly, I thought I'd love it. Be someone else for a while? It sounded like a lot of fun, especially since I'm a naturally shy person, and it's easier to pretend than be myself. But I hadn't counted on the never-ending suspense and fear."

Shira looks into Eliana's eyes and sees genuine interest, and concern. It really helps to be able to let down her guard with somebody who might empathize, a luxury she doesn't have with Ari, or any of her fellow agents.

Do the other agents feel the same way? She asks herself. *I doubt it. They're guys. They're bullet-proof. But I suppose that, at some level, they have feelings too. It's just that they're hard-wired not to show it.*

"What are the Khans like?" Eliana asks, breaking into Shira's thoughts.

"Surprisingly normal, and nice."

"Even Mr. Khan? It seems like he would be hardened by the circumstances."

"He's pretty reticent to talk about any of that," Shira answers. "I'm sure he has his emotional battle scars. But, deep down, I think he's actually a sweet man."

"I haven't heard Arab men described that way before."

"Don't get me wrong, Eliana," Shira replies. "He rules the roost. If anybody disobeys him, he'll come down hard."

"The same with a lot of Jewish men I know," Eliana adds.

"But his love for his family and his dedication to his work are apparent. He's a good man."

"Lucky for you."

"Just to be clear," Shira quickly clarifies. "I'm scared to death of him. He's smart, suspicious, and can undoubtedly be cruel when he has to be. Especially, I suspect, with an Israeli spy. So, I have to be very careful."

"How does he feel about Jews in general?" Eliana asks.

"A lot like we feel about Arabs," Shira responds. "I don't think he knows any Jews personally, but, if he did, he would never like or trust us. Still, there's a begrudging respect for our ability to fight. I remember him saying one time, 'Underestimate a Jew at your own risk.'"

"Probably true."

"Actually, Eliana, I'd be careful about stereotyping anybody," Shira counters. "If there's one thing I've learned by living with the Kahn's, it's that all of us, no matter our religion, race, or customs, are more alike than we realize. We all just want to live our life as we see fit."

"But they will never leave us alone," Eliana counters. "That's why we need you out there doing the dirty work. And, I hear, you're excelling at that. Mazel Tov."

Chapter 7
Uganda

Shira gazes out the window at a cloud-obscured landscape. So far, her flight to Entebbe has gone as planned. But not as she had hoped. She wanted the hostage situation resolved before she arrived. Her fondest wish was that she could arrive, then, hop right back onto a plane back. Unfortunately, no such luck.

In fact, not only is the hostage situation still unresolved but, when Shira lands, she's told that the hijackers are now saying that if their demands aren't met, they will begin killing hostages on July 1.

Not totally unexpected, probably. Hijackers always demand and threaten. But it makes Shira's assignment, which was hardly routine to begin with, way more complicated.

What if they kill the pilot first, she thinks. *Will I be forced into a public showing of grief that will expose me as an imposter? Will I be arrested by the Ugandan army?*

But first things first. Her biggest problem is what to do now that they've landed. She's in her seat, on the plane, sitting on the tarmac, with no papers and no instructions of any kind. A kind of helpless position if she's interrogated when she departs.

But, fortunately, before any passenger is let off the plane, an official-looking woman comes on board, spots Shira, and hands her a package, saying she had been told to deliver it as soon as the plane landed.

The package contains papers confirming Shira's identity as a French nationalist married to the pilot of the hijacked plane. Shira takes a quick look and everything looks authentic, including the letter of introduction, and the French passport. But, of course, it really isn't, which, hopefully, nobody notices.

The picture on the passport is deliberately blurred and aged, making it difficult to tell exactly how old she is. And, with the creases and wrinkles meticulously added to her face and hands by makeup artists back in Tel Aviv, Shira looks amazingly similar to the photo.

It might work, she thinks.

But, as it turns out, she needn't have worried. When she deplanes nobody looks at her, or her papers, or anything else.

The few Ugandan troops scattered about are too busy with reporters and government officials to check the ID's of newly arriving family members. So, with less scrutiny than she would get at any airport in the world, Shira joins the other passengers on the tarmac, where they wait for a few minutes, before they're loaded onto a bus to the terminal. Once there, Shira's small group joins the other relatives that are standing by in an adjoining room, waiting, and hoping, for their loved ones to be released.

Most are Israeli, and speaking Hebrew, so Shira understands what's being said. However, not wanting to risk exposure she stays in character, not easy to do when all around her questions are being asked that she could easily answer. Playing dumb is not one of Shira's strong suits.

There are no officials around anywhere. Which is surprising. Maybe it's because resources are scarce, or the relatives aren't considered dangerous, or the guards are just that incompetent. Whatever the reason, the group is left alone and so, without fear of detection, Shira is able to sit down and look over her "official" papers.

She finds instructions from Ari that are a little more demanding than she expected. She's to interview hostages as soon as they are released. Questions are suggested but, obviously, anything she can learn about the hijackers will be helpful.

More importantly, she needs to document anything about the physical spaces of the terminal that might prove useful in a raid. Any skylights? Location of doors? Where the guards are stationed?

Instinctively, Shira looks around the room she's in, trying to see identifying features. It's pretty nondescript. Might have even been a small hangar at one time. She can't tell where the hostages are located, or even if they're in the same building. She just knows they aren't here.

She sees no restrooms anywhere, and thinks that may be her ticket into other areas of the terminal, where she can gather more usable intel. As she plots her strategy, though, her thinking is interrupted by somebody calling out her new name.

"Madame Bacos," she hears. "Madame Rosemary Bacos, please identify yourself."

The loud voice is coming from a bullhorn held by a young black man in uniform. Shira doesn't really know whether he's military or police but, given that anybody in uniform is dangerous to her right now, that hardly matters. For some reason she's been singled out. That can't be good.

She raises her hand tentatively, then identifies herself to the guard, and nervously hands over her passport. The Ugandan looks at her picture, and at her face, then, gives the passport back without comment. First test passed.

He leads Shira across the waiting room to a small, closed door on the other side of the room where, after knocking only once, he escorts her inside. She finds herself in a tiny office, occupied by a small and angry-faced Ugandan, who is sitting at a desk appropriately matched to his size.

His head is down, but a jagged scar is visible on his right cheek, making him look more menacing. And his plump belly speaks to his status. Unlike some of his countrymen, it's obvious this guy hasn't missed many meals.

Finally, after pausing long enough to make Shira as uncomfortable as possible, the man looks up and in French, introduces himself as Major Odoki.

Then, he asks to see her papers.

Does he suspect something? Shira thinks. *Could my cover be blown so quickly? And, if so, what will he do with me? Looking at the guy, it can't be good.*

But Shira's concerns are misplaced. Major Odoki isn't unfriendly or suspicious at all. Quite the opposite, in fact. Once he's reviewed everything, the Major looks up at her with a smile on his face, which, in a strange way, makes him even more terrifying.

He tells Shira that he has singled her out specifically today to update her on the status of the hostages in general, and her husband in particular.

"Just doing my job," he says in French.

He tells her that the hijackers have divided the hostages into two groups, those that are Israeli and those that are not.

"We're expecting the non-Israelis to be released fairly soon," he says, looking disconcertedly over her left shoulder and not right at her, "but, at this point, we don't know about the Jewish hostages."

"What about the crew?" Shira asks, realizing that, if the pilot is released, her cover could be blown sooner rather than later. Not a good thing.

"Originally, they were going to be released as well," Odoki continues, " but I have unfortunate news for you. Your husband has chosen to stay with the hostages."

Shira hides her relief and as best she can, looks distraught.

"Why would he do that?"

"Evidently, it's a matter of honor. Going down with his ship or some such," the officer answers, minimizing the courage of the pilot. "I'm sorry. You must be terribly disappointed."

"Does he know I'm here?"

"Not yet. We wanted to talk to you first."

Shira calls on her meager acting skills, as she ponders the question, first looking at the ceiling, then the floor. Finally, she looks directly into the man's eyes and says, "It's probably best he not know at this point"

"I agree. Why complicate the situation," the Ugandan replies, "or, even worse, risk getting you involved?"

Oh, I'm involved, Shira thinks, *and fortunately, you don't know how much.*

"Can I see where they're being held?" She asks. "It would help me deal with the fear, and uncertainty. I'll feel better if I can confirm that my husband is safe."

"I'm afraid not," the officer says. "But, when you go out of my office, just look down the corridor to your right. At the end are two parallel doors. Behind them is a large room where the hostages are being housed. Your husband is perfectly safe. I can promise you that."

"Are there windows I can look through? Or any other way to see Michel? I just want to make sure he's OK."

"No. There are no windows that you can look through," the Major answers with a sardonic smile, "but when, and if, any hostages are released, you can be part of the group greeting them if you like."

"Yes. I would like that," Shira replies.

Major Odoki nods, and goes back to shuffling papers.

Shira slowly realizes she's been dismissed and rising from her chair, glances back at the officer's paperwork, hoping to pick up some tidbit of significance. But she can't really see anything. So, Shira calls out to the guard to escort her back to the other family members.

On the way back, however, she glances at the two doors leading to the room where dozens of scared, tired, and hungry hostages are awaiting their fate.

Hopefully, a raid won't be necessary, she thinks. *It could turn into a bloodbath.*

****

"Please wake up, Madame Bacos. Major Odoki would like to see you. He has news about the hostages." It's the young Ugandan soldier again trying to be as polite as possible.

Shira is curled up in the corner of the waiting room on a blanket she brought with her for just such an occasion. It has been a rough night and she is being awakened from the only deep sleep she was able to get all night. She glances at her watch. It's 7:30 a.m.

There are just a few people in the room with her. Most of the others must have found sleeping accommodations elsewhere. Maybe in buses brought in for that purpose. Or perhaps at homes in town. But Shira opted to stay at the airport just in case some hostages were released during the night. Maybe that's the news that Major Odoki wants to share with her now.

"What kind of news?" she asks as she sits up and rubs the sleep out of her eyes.

"I'm not sure," he replies. "But Major Odoki asked me to bring you to him right away. He seems quite excited."

The walk back to the office is not as long as Shira remembered from the night before. But maybe that's because she's not as nervous. She's either adapting to the situation, or just anticipating good news. Or oblivious to the danger that lies ahead.

Shira glances over at the two doors again. As far as she can tell, nothing has changed there. No government officials are around. No reporters. Or cameramen. And no indication of any kind that hostages might be released anytime soon. So, maybe it isn't good news after all.

Major Odoki greets Shira outside the office, with a grin on his face, and shakes her hand enthusiastically. He ushers her through his open door and motions for her to sit down.

For some reason he seems quite pleased with himself as he circles the desk and plumps down in his leather chair. He sits up erect, the broad smile still splitting his face into two halves. Other than the scar, which is clearly visible, there's no sign of the menacing man who had confronted her the evening before.

An idle thought occurs to Shira. Maybe he was just playing a role yesterday, trying to intimidate her, just as she is playing a role, trying to make him believe she's the pilot's wife. Maybe they are both imposters. Or maybe, and more likely, her lack of sleep has made her a touch delusional.

The Major continues to beam triumphantly for a few seconds, then leans in and says in a whisper, "Madam Bacos, I have good news for you."

Well, get on with it, she thinks.

But he won't be hurried. Finally, after leaning back in his chair a bit, fingers intertwined behind his head, he continues, still in a soft voice, "I am pleased to inform you that the hijackers have begun to secretly release a few passengers to us. They are gathered in another room, over there, on the other side of the terminal. No government officials have been told and the press doesn't know yet."

"That's incredible," Shira says. "When will the hostages be able to leave?"

"I'm told that people are working on the logistics as we speak. But I believe that those released today will be on a plane to Paris tonight."

"How many will be released?"

"Around fifty. All the non-Israelis," he answers.

"And my husband?" Shira asks.

"Not sure. But I think he's still planning to stay with the remaining hostages."

"So, I'm curious. Why are you telling me this now, ahead of anybody else?" Shira asks.

"Because one of the hostages being released asked to speak to you by name," he replies. "I'm not sure why but she may be your best chance to learn more about your husband's intentions."

"So will I be able to meet with her?"

"Of course. I'll bring her to you right now."

Shira looks around the room while she waits.

Like everything in this one-story, pre-fab Entebbe airport it is spartan. Just a table and two chairs. No other furnishings or fixtures of any kind. The good thing is that, best Shira can tell, there's no place to hide a camera or listening device, so she and the hostage will be totally alone.

Shira wonders who the hostage is and why she singled out the pilot's wife to meet with alone. Surely, she doesn't know about Shira. But it is suspicious. First Shira's singled out by the officer in charge, twice in fact, and now, she's been asked to meet with one of the first hostages to be released. Something just doesn't smell right.

A small, disheveled, and dark-haired woman enters the room and sits down, her eyes averted. Everything about her is modest and non-threatening. So far so good.

Shira extends her hand and after a few seconds of hesitation, the woman grips it firmly, then looks right into Shira's eyes, still holding on. In contrast to her rather mousy first impression, the woman's eyes are now surprisingly alert, confident, and she speaks first.

"Madam Bacos," she says in French, "so pleased to meet you. I'm Ninette Morenu. Your husband sends his best, although, frankly, he was very surprised to hear you were here in person. Last he heard, you were in Canada, tending to your sister. How is she, by the way?"

"Much improved," Shira improvises. "I just felt that being here for Michel was more important at this point. How are you handling everything?"

"Much better now. It was pretty harrowing for a while."

"And Michel?"

"Given the circumstances, he's fine." the freed woman says. "He's the stalwart leader you know him to be, and frankly, I don't know what the rest of us would have done without him."

"Not surprising."

"I bring a message from him by the way," Ninette says looking around. "But, first, do you think we're being watched or recorded?"

"Not that I can tell. I don't see anywhere to hide a device," Shira responds. "What's the message?"

"Well, to start with, Michel's wife doesn't have a sister," Ninette says. "So, there's that."

The color drains from Shira's face. *Who is this woman? Who sent her? And what does she want?*

"So, obviously, you're not Michel's wife," Ninette says. "And the question is, who are you? I'm guessing you work for the Israeli government. Probably sent here to sort things out, although, frankly, I'm surprised they would send somebody so young on such an important mission."

So much for the disguise, and for the alias as well. All of a sudden, she feels naked, and incredibly alone. Oh, and this woman doesn't look mousy any more.

"But the good news is that I'm on your side." Ninette goes on. "I was released by the hijackers because of my French name. But I'm every bit as Jewish as you are."

Welcome news for Shira, if it's true.

"How can I believe you?" she asks cautiously.

"Other than my name and my French passport, I can't prove anything to you right now, can I? But, frankly, what does it hurt to listen?" Ninette answers.

"Good point."

"So, I have two things that can be helpful to you," Ninette explains. "First, I've been sitting in that room with the hostages for a couple of days now with nothing to do but stare at the walls, and the roof, and the windows, and the guards. And second, I have a photographic memory."

Shira is taken aback. Who is this angel of mercy?

I have one major assignment, she thinks, *to find out everything I can about this terminal, and evidently, this Ninette person has memorized all of it. And is highly motivated to share it. Can I be this lucky? Or is something fishy?*

A few minutes later, with her potential angel of mercy now properly equipped with paper and pencil, Shira just sits back and watches as the Israeli with the French-sounding name produces a fully actionable map out of thin air.

She describes the rooms, yes, but also where the hostages are located, and the guards, and what doors are best for Israeli soldiers to enter and exit. She even points out where the light fixtures are, in case somebody wants to shoot them out.

And, when the diagram is finished, Ninette hands it to Shira, who folds it up and tucks it into her tote bag. She plans to guard it with her life because so many innocent lives may depend on her getting it into the right hands.

She tearfully hugs her benefactor, and for the time being, they part ways. Then, Shira heads directly to the office of Major Odoki to tell him that she needs to be on the next plane out. She makes up a story about a family emergency at home and teary-eyed, says she has to leave with the hostages that are being released.

But her dramatic scene isn't necessary. The Major informs her that all family members will be leaving with the released hostages. Evidently, it is getting too dangerous for them to remain at the airport. So, Shira wires Ari a cryptic message, "I'm on a charter flight to Paris. With hostages that were released. Hope to see you there and discuss the trip."

Finally, she gets on the plane, inconspicuous among the celebratory freed hostages, and flies away, hoping it's the last she ever sees of the shabby Entebbe Airport, the portly Major Odoki, and the incredibly corrupt government of Idi Amin.

Chapter 8
Paris

The charter flight lands at Orly Airport in Paris at 6:15 a.m. in the morning.

Despite the early time, the plane is met by a large crowd of reporters and officials, all anxious to learn anything they can about the hostage situation. With neither side willing to compromise, and tensions rising exponentially, the public interest and concern for the hostages has increased dramatically.

Shira hopes that somewhere in the hubbub of the terminal her contact is waiting. With Ninette in tow, she pushes her way through dozens of reporters, all desperately trying to get information any way they can.

Flash bulbs pop. Questions are shouted at nobody in particular, and never answered. If any of the passengers seem about to say something, they are assaulted immediately by microphones.

"How many hostages have been released? How many are left? Who are the hijackers? What kind of deal do they want?"

It's apparent that Shira and Ninette will not, or cannot, answer their questions. So, the reporters move on, their microphones held in front of them like weapons, looking for somebody more cooperative. A few of the hostages do speak, if only to capture their fifteen minutes of fame, but most do not.

Eventually, Shira is freed up enough to scan the crowd for the face of her contact, but, given that she has no idea what he looks like, or even if he's there, her chances of spotting him are negligible.

If Ari sent somebody, the guy must know what I look like, Shira tells herself, *from a photo or something.*

So, she stands on a bench to be more visible when, fortunately, she sees a sign way at the back of the crowd with the pilot's wife's name on.

There he is, she thinks. *Pretty subtle to use my alias. So subtle I almost missed it.*

Shira hops down, grabs Ninette's arm, and together, they push their way through the crowd, toward the sign. When they get there, they see it's being held by a nondescript, puffy-faced middle-aged man, somebody who would never stand out in a crowd this size. Typical Mossad maneuver.

Why can't they ever send somebody tall, dark, and handsome? Shira says to herself. *I'd have a much better chance of spotting him in a crowd.*

But, as she thinks about it, she hasn't seen many of those in the Mossad anyway. She guesses most good-looking guys become insurance agents, or travel agents, not federal agents like Ari.

"Hi, Shira. I'm Harold," the man says in a squeaky voice. "Follow me. I've secured an office where we can be alone."

Once all three people are crammed into the small office space, Harold seems to fade into the woodwork and Ninette takes charge again.

She spreads out her map on the desk and scribbles on it as she talks. Her memory is clicking off images and thoughts faster than her mind can decipher them, proving that Ninette indeed does have a photographic memory. And, when asked a question, she closes her eyes briefly, then answers in intricate detail, leaving nothing to the imagination.

Harold is writing things down as quickly as he can but Ninette's mind is moving at warp speed, which is even more surprising given that she hasn't had any sleep. She keeps going back to fill in details and add things that, on the surface, may seem meaningless, but really aren't. Like where the light switches are, or what walls are load-bearing or, even, who needs to be taken out first.

The map is covered with notes, all in Hebrew, and all important to anybody planning a raid. Eventually, though, Ninette hits a wall. Her eyelids droop, her computer mind shuts down, and Harold wisely calls it a day.

"You're booked into a hotel near here. I'll take you there and we'll finish up tomorrow morning," he says. "You've been incredibly helpful, Ninette. When this ordeal is over, you'll be appropriately thanked, and rewarded."

"What about me?" Shira asks sarcastically.

Harold looks at her quizzically and says, "Your reward is keeping your job."

"No, I mean, do I have a hotel room? Can I get some rest, too?"

"I'm sorry. I thought Ari told you. You're booked on an afternoon flight back to Tel Aviv. They want to de-brief you as soon as possible and then, send you on your way."

"On my way to where?" Shira asks.

"Back to Beirut, of course," he answers, "to be with your family. Oh, and thanks for your help, but we'll take it from here."

Chapter 9
Tel Aviv

Ari is sporting a rarely seen grin that makes him look like the cross between a gremlin and a village idiot.

He's at the front of a large briefing room brimming with government officials, most of whom are not Mossad.

Ari is the only one who's smiling because the purpose of the meeting is deadly serious. It is to begin preparations for a raid on the Entebbe Airport that will, hopefully, free the hostages still imprisoned there.

Ari has been milling about, proud as a peacock because he's to start the meeting by introducing Shira, who's there to describe the scene at Entebbe Airport, as well as to present Ninette's map and notes to the assembled dignitaries.

After shaking as many hands as he can, Ari begins the meeting by recognizing a few luminaries, starting with the Prime Minister, then launches into an introduction of his prize recruit.

"So, Shira was able to befriend the Major in charge of the airport," he says, "and to convince him that she needed to see a woman named Ninette Morenu before anybody else did."

"Actually, Ninette asked for me," Shira corrects her boss.

"What?"

"Ninette asked to see me," she goes on, "because she had guessed I was an Israeli undercover agent."

"Well, whatever," Ari said, "the thing is that Ms. Abelson went undercover into a very hostile environment. Then, she convinced the officials in charge that she was harmless, found the one hostage who could help us, and produced the map you see displayed on the screen."

Shira rolls her eyes. Ari is going stick to his narrative and it probably doesn't help Shira to keep correcting him. Just the opposite, in fact. So, she remains quiet.

"I give you Shira Abelson."

Ari concludes with a flourish rarely seen from a Mossad official. He's flushed, sweating, and still beaming, like a Cheshire cat.

As Shira rises to speak, it dawns on her just how much Ari has invested in her, and why he has been moving her along so quickly. He wants to showcase her skills, yes, but, also, he wants to validate his risky decision to bring her on board.

Hiring a man would've carried little risk. Everybody does that and there were many to choose from. But a young woman? Who's head strong like she is ? And lacking the normal qualifications?

Shira realizes that Ari has a lot riding on her, and she better not blow it, not only for herself, but for him as well. Still, Shira feels remarkably calm standing in front of such a distinguished audience of government officials.

You've got this, girl, she says to herself. *Compared to Beirut or Entebbe, this isn't that tough. And, as Eliana counseled me, I should welcome the challenge, have fun with it, and if I wash out, so be it. I can always go back to being a doctor.*

"First, I'd like to say that we're very lucky that Ninette Morenu was even released," Shira begins. "By marriage, she has a French name but she's every bit as Jewish as the rest of us. Fortunately, the hijackers didn't dig deeply enough into her background to know that."

There's a little rustling in the room. Some are done with the introductions already. They're anxious to get on with the main event, and the map is illuminated behind Shira, just waiting to be explained.

Too bad, Shira says to herself. *I'm going to give Ninette her due. And make Ari proud in the process.*

"More importantly," Shira continues, "she's a passionate patriot who, from the start, knew the role she could play, and used her photographic memory to give us details the rest of us might have missed."

Shira turns toward the slide projected on the screen, pointer in hand. A glance back convinces her she has everybody's full attention.

"What you see here is a map that Ninette sketched out for us at Entebbe," she says. "The notes are hers, often in response to questions, or to amplify a point she wanted to make. Granted, she's hardly qualified to plan a raid, but still, some things were pretty obvious to her."

Shira pauses again, half expecting interruptions. But everybody is busy trying to understand the map and read the notes scribbled in the margins. Their eyes are squinted, facial expressions serious, and you could hear a pin drop in the room.

"They're keeping the hostages together," Shira goes on, "which should make a raid easier, especially if we can surprise them in the middle of the night. And the hostages are guarded by only three men. Obviously, those guys need to be taken out first, and then, the leadership next."

"Not your decision."

The comment is murmured and it isn't immediately clear to Shira who said it. Probably Lt. General Dan Shamron, the uniformed guy to Shira's left, who Ari told her would be in charge of the raid.

But she isn't sure of that. It could have been one of the bureaucrats sitting near him. Still, caution being a big part of valor, she answers, "Fair enough. I'll keep my thoughts to myself. Any questions?"

The next hour or so is filled with a lot of give-and-take on how to proceed. As the discussion goes on, Shira sits back down and other people take the stage to argue their point of view. And, eventually, Ari and Shira are excused from the meeting entirely.

No "thank you" or "job well done," from anybody. But Ari is giddy, which is enough reward for her.

"Great job," he says. "We're going to have to gather up some of the original airport architectural drawings and probably do some air reconnaissance before deciding on next steps."

"Anything more I can do?"

"No. Just go home and pack. Tomorrow, you'll fly back to Beirut and pick up right where you left off. I took the

95

liberty of letting the Kahn family know you were coming, by the way. Hope you don't mind."

"Of course, I mind, boss. How about a few days off every now and then," Shira counters.

"You can rest in Beirut"

"Have you been to Beirut lately?"

"Shira, I know we're working you pretty hard," Ari acknowledges. "But we want to understand the political situation in Lebanon better than we do right now. You're firmly embedded there, trusted by Majed and in the long run, I think what you do in Beirut will be more important than anything you did at Entebbe. And that's saying something."

With that, Ari dismisses his most important asset by just turning around, and walking away. No handshake. No hug. No anything.

But Shira doesn't mind. She knows how proud he is of her.

When Shira gets home, she's surprised to find a note from Aaron, posted on the door of her apartment.

"Where are you?" It reads. "I miss you. Please call me," followed by his number. No time. No date. It could have been there for days, or weeks. Who knows?

The last time they spoke, she told Aaron that she never wanted to see him again. It was a lie, of course, forced by her boss's ultimatum that she cut all personal ties with him. But Aaron bought it, for a while at least.

Yet his note speaks to a change of heart. And it couldn't be more timely. Now that things have turned so positive for her at the agency, that she's earned her chops, so to speak, Shira has been thinking about reaching out to Aaron as well.

And she knows Ari would be hesitant to give her the same kind of ultimatum in the future, no matter what the scuttlebutt is about Aaron fraternizing with their Arab enemies.

So, without hesitation, she returns Aaron's call and they agree to meet that very afternoon in a park a few blocks from her apartment house. She's excited to see Aaron again and as she approaches the park, she's as nervous as she was on their first date, and her heart is fluttering like a schoolgirl's.

When she sees Aaron, however, her nervousness disappears, and she realizes how much she missed him. He's comfortable and familiar, like the old friend he is, and instinctively, she runs to him, throws her arms around his neck, and gives him a long kiss that leaves little doubt about how happy she is to see him.

"Aaron, what a wonderful surprise," she says. "I'm so glad you called."

They sit down, hold hands, and begin to talk. She learns that Aaron is still trying to save the world, one diplomatic meeting at a time. And he finds out that Shira has some kind of sales job that takes her all over the world.

At least, that's what she says.

When he starts to ask more questions, she interrupts the discussion with another kiss, and says, "Let's go back to my place. We can talk more there."

When they do get to her apartment house, however, talking takes a back seat to other, more immediate, things. At the inner door, Shira rummages through her purse for her keys, fumbles a bit trying to fit the right one into the lock, and then, pulls him inside for another embrace, this one more passionate.

They start up the stairs, hand in hand, walking briskly, then, breaking into a run, taking steps two at a time, giggling all the way like the kids they really still are. Shira is reminded of the wonderful times they had when they were in school together.

Again, at her door, the keys slow them down briefly, but, once inside the apartment, everything starts flying off them, his shoes into the corner, her skirt over the couch, and a rumpled trail of clothes leading directly to the bed.

"That must a world record for making it into bed," Aaron quips, as he climbs gently on top of Shira, pulling the sheet over both of them.

"Slow down, big boy. We don't have to hurry anymore."

But her words have little effect. Aaron sees, or perhaps more appropriately, feels what he wants, and nothing will stop him now.

"Oh well," Shira says a minute later. "Fortunately, we have all night to get it right."

As they lay beside each other, the questions that Shira is curious about, but didn't ask earlier, start to tumble out.

"How did you find me?" she asks.

"Ran into a girlfriend of yours," Aaron answers. "She wasn't sure you were still living here but right there, on the directory, in the entryway, there was your name, big as life. I talked my way in and left the note on your door."

"I'm glad you did."

"I wasn't sure you'd call. You were so insistent that we not see each other again."

"Temporary insanity," Shira explains. "I'm over it now."

"Well," Aaron says. "You might have lost your mind, but you still have your looks."

"I doubt that. Especially after the last few weeks. But, thank you for saying that."

"No. I'm serious. You look great. Whatever you've been doing obviously appeals to you," Aaron counters. "What kind of sales job is it, by the way?"

Shira sits up a little, shifts the pillow behind her head, and starts to speak, seemingly oblivious to her nakedness and the impact it's having on Aaron.

"I sell female products," she lies, knowing full well that topic should cut off any follow-up questions. And it does.

Eventually she will have to tell the "somebody in her life" what she really does for a living. But Aaron hardly qualifies for that role yet. And, of course, given that he's still a persona non grata at the agency, and they have such strict rules about relationships, her lying will have to continue for the time being.

"So how are things between us and our good Muslim friends these days?" She asks, changing the subject.

"Pretty frustrating," he answers. "I can see both sides. And, if I'm being totally honest, it's easier working with the Arabs sometimes than it is with our government, who can be so secretive, and rigid."

Shira knows that better than Aaron does. But it is still a bit disconcerting to hear him voice any support for Israel's archenemies. Especially given what Eliana told her.

Still, she doesn't want to start an argument at this fragile stage of their rekindled romance. So, to avoid that, and because she is still feeling very warm and adventurous, Shira effectively changes the subject by fondling Aaron toward another arousal that eventually satisfies their ardor.

Then, they fall fast asleep.

At 6:30 a.m. Aaron wakes up and reaches over to the other side of the bed hoping Shira is still there. The covers are rumpled, the sheets still warm, but he's all alone.

He listens for sounds of somebody padding about, a toilet flushing, perhaps. But Shira has vanished again. *Back into the world of what was it? Feminine products? Hardly.*

As Aaron puts on his clothes, now stacked neatly on a chair in the corner of the bedroom, he notices a note propped up against the lamp on Shira's desk. It says, in carefully written block letters:

A.

IT WAS GRAND. I'M OFF ON ANOTHER ADVENTURE. PLEASE LOCK UP AND I'LL SEE YOU WHEN I SEE YOU.

S.

Typical Shira breeziness, he thinks, *written without a hint of warmth, or love. But she is what she is. And I love her for it.*

Chapter 10
Beirut

Surprisingly, Raya is waiting for Shira in the Beirut Airport arrival area. Obviously, Ari let the family know when she would arrive, and on what flight. Still, it's unusual for a young girl, any woman for that matter, to come alone to this airport, one of the most dangerous spots in Beirut.

Shira's even more surprised by the warmth the Kahn daughter shows her as she exits. After embracing Shira as if she were a family member, Raya holds her hand and guides her through the throngs of passengers just milling about, all of whom are trying to find some way, any way, to get out of Beirut.

As an Israeli, Shira naturally feels some responsibility for the troubles these people are experiencing. The creation of the state of Israel was largely responsible for the displacement of hundreds of thousands of Palestinian refugees into Lebanon, shifting the demographic balance of the country dramatically.

And, then, once in the majority, those Lebanese Muslims became unhappy with their Christian political leaders, and their protests eventually led to a civil war.

"What were you doing in Tel Aviv?" Raya asks innocently.

"Just a stopover," Shira improvises. "I ran into some old friends in Paris who were going there, and I joined them. First time for me. You ever been there?"

"No. I don't think I want to either."

"It's a nice city but I get it," Shira says. "As an American, I'm sure they treat me differently than they would you."

"You got that right."

"How're things here?" Shira asks as they load her luggage into Raya's car. It's a sincere question. Things change quickly in Beirut, and it's been a few weeks.

"Still sporadic fighting. Rumors of another ceasefire," Raya answers. "But, given that none have worked in the past, few are optimistic."

"How's your father holding up?"

"OK, I guess," Raya answers. "Sarkis still hasn't been inaugurated so nobody's sure who's really in charge. Prime Minister Karami is filling the void best he can, but honestly, it isn't working very well at the moment. And I'm afraid for my father. He tries to remain neutral in the political battles but I doubt his job is any safer because of it. Hard to tell what side anybody is on these days."

Shira studies Raya's face as the young girl drives carefully through the narrow, sometimes rutted, and mostly filthy streets of her home town. The strain of living in a war zone is obviously having its effect on her. The poor girl seems to have aged a year or two in just the short time Shira's been gone.

Raya should be thinking about grades, sports, and boys but, instead, she worries that her father might not come home one day, or that her family will have to flee Lebanon, or that a random shell will find their home, and destroy it.

It probably isn't good for a spy to have empathy, Shira thinks, *but I can't exactly wall off my feelings, can I?*

"I'm surprised you were able to get back in here," Raya says. "I heard that the Americans cancelled all student visas and work permits."

Oh shit, Shira thinks. *What if Ari missed that little news flash. And what if my cover gets blown right off the bat.*

"Obviously that's not true," Shira bluffs, "or I wouldn't be here, would I?"

The next morning Peggy (aka Shira) pretends to sleep in, just so she won't have to see Majed. She wants to put off any inquisition as long as possible, especially now that there might be a glitch in her cover story.

He will know about the cancellation of American student visas, of course, and he won't be as gullible as Raya. He'll ask questions she might find hard to answer.

So, after her normal morning walk, when Raya and her mother are at the market for their daily shopping, Shira calls Ari.

"Nothing I can tell you about Entebbe," he answers cryptically.

"Any more hostages released?"

"Nothing I can tell you."

"Well, surely you'll tell me this. Is my husband OK?"

"Shira, knock it off."

So, she switches to the subject of the American travel ban, and on that front, Ari has some good news. He tells her that the American restrictions were never officially put in place and because of the ceasefire, Ari doesn't expect them to be anytime soon. So, that problem is averted, at least for the moment.

"But, isn't it risky for me to stay here?" she asks Ari. "What if they do put the restrictions in? And what if Majed starts to ask questions about why an American would come back here anyway, in the middle of this mess."

"Listen, Shira, you're the only resource we have in Beirut at the moment," Ari explains, "and any information you can gather for us is too valuable to just throw away because you're getting nervous. In fact, I've been getting questions from my bosses already about when your reports will start up again."

"I doubt I'll have much to report," Shira counters. "Certainly nothing that would be worth the risk I'm taking."

"I'll be the judge of that. Listen, if worse comes to worst, if the Americans restrict travel or something like that, you can always make up some story about dual citizenship, show them your French passport, and get out of there."

"I'm sure that sounds like a good plan to you, sitting in your comfy chair, behind your big desk there in Tel Aviv," Shira responds sarcastically, "but here in Beirut, with an inquisitive Majed breathing down my neck, it doesn't sound so good to me."

"Well, then, now that you're a full-fledged Mossad agent, just come up with a better one."

Then, Ari hangs up.

Shira is angry and scared, a lethal combination, but she has little time to be either. She takes a quick tour around the house and confirms it's empty. Then, she sits down on her bed to think. But, instead, she starts to cry.

Big, heaving sobs interrupted only by gasps as she tries to get enough air into her lungs to cry again. She collapses across the bed coverings and tries unsuccessfully to muffle the cries in a pillow.

The pressure of the last few days, the lack of sleep, the worry about being stuck in probably the most troubled city in all the world. It's all crashing down on her suddenly. And she feels so alone.

In fact, this is the first time in days that she's been able to let her emotions out. Nobody is around. It's the perfect time to take off the mask she's been wearing and let the scared little girl emerge, if only for a few minutes.

And who knows, she thinks, *when I can actually let my hair down again.*

Which sets off a fresh wave of tears. *I wish I had somebody to confide in,* she tells herself, *like Eliana. But she's not here. Nobody's here. Just me. Only me. Even Ari has turned against me.*

And then, surprisingly, as her face muscles relax, and her chest stops heaving and her eyes dry up, she begins to feel better. Not just better, in fact, incredibly better, and confident again. She feels her grit and determination coming back.

I don't know who that blubbering mess was a few seconds ago, she tells herself, *but it certainly wasn't me. I'm a trained professional, ready and able to do my job.*

Just then, she hears the front door open.

"Peggy, we're home," Raya cries out.

So much for rehearsing answers and planning her strategy. Once again, Shira will have to wing it.

That night, at dinner, even after what must surely have been a hectic and grueling day, Majed has enough energy to give Shira the grilling she has been expecting.

"Raya tells me you were in Tel Aviv," he starts.

"Yes, I was. Just a stopover."

"From where?"

"I was in Paris visiting friends. A relative of one of my girlfriends was getting married there," Shira starts to weave her impromptu tale, not really sure where it will go.

"You have a girlfriend living in Paris?"

"No, actually she lives in Cleveland, uh, the U.S., but her aunt got married there," she stammers. "Pretty extravagant from what I hear."

"Did you like Tel Aviv?" he asks.

"Didn't spend enough time there to like or dislike it. I had dinner with friends at a restaurant near the hotel. The food was pretty mediocre, by the way. Then, I flew out the next day."

"I don't like kosher food that much myself," Majed volunteers.

Or anything else Jewish, I suspect, Shira thinks. *The Muslims may be fighting Christians here in Beirut but Jews are their real enemy.*

"How are things here, Majed? Think the ceasefire will hold?" Shira tries goes on the offensive.

"Doubt it. But I suppose it's worth a try."

"Is there something you guys can do to turn it into a lasting peace?"

Majed sighs, and then says, "Look, Peggy. Syrian troops are in our country fighting the Palestinians. We're like bystanders. There are random killings in Beirut every day. Nobody knows who's shooting whom, or for what reason."

"Not even a top official like you?"

"Especially me. I don't even know where our elected President is at the moment. Can you believe that? All I know is that he hasn't been inaugurated yet. And the old President still acts like he's in charge. Which isn't a good thing. For the country or me."

Shira wishes she could take notes as Majed rants.

"Many of our people want us to deploy our military without even knowing who the enemy is. Bottom-line, I'm afraid we have little control of our country, and it'll be a killing ground for some time to come."

Finally, he averts his eyes and with a surprisingly sweet smile, asks, "What was your question again?"

Shira's tactic has worked. Majed's interrogation of her is over. But not the uneasiness about her situation.

****

"Peggy, wake up. You won't believe what happened last night."

It takes a moment for Shira to remember where she is, who Peggy is, and another minute to register what's being said to her.

"The Israelis freed the hostages being held in Entebbe."

Shira rubs the sleep out of her eyes and tries to grasp the significance of what Raya is telling her. It worked. All the planning must have paid off.

"They raided the airport at Entebbe last night," Raya goes on, "and freed the hostages."

"Anybody killed?" Shira asks, now totally awake.

"From what we hear, all of the hijackers were killed and lots of Ugandan soldiers as well." Raya answers. "I'm not sure how many Israelis. A few I think."

"How many hostages survived?"

"Almost all. The Israelis are calling the raid a huge success but, of course, they would say that no matter what, right?"

Shira agrees. If she wants a truly professional assessment of the raid, she will need to call Ari as soon as possible. But, for now, Raya is her only source of information.

"What else do you know?"

"I guess the Israeli who was in charge of the raid was killed. Shot on the tarmac. Some guy named Netanyahu."

By now Shira is sitting straight up in the bed. It takes all of her willpower to stay calm. She doesn't want to tip her hand but there's so much she'd like to know. For now, though, it's prudent to keep any more probing to herself, at least until she can talk to her boss.

"So, how do you feel about it?" she asks Raya.

"Mixed emotions. The Israelis can be bullies at times but I'm really glad the hostages are safe."

"I agree. Innocent people shouldn't be caught up in all of this stuff."

Raya looks at Shira strangely, then responds, with just the hint of an attitude.

"That's the thing about you Americans, Peggy. You still think there's such a thing as innocent people."

"What do you mean?"

"If people elect leaders who start wars, are they innocent?" Raya explains. "If people don't care enough to understand what's going on, are they innocent?"

Shira is a bit taken aback by the intensity of Raya's words. It's a side of her Shira hasn't seen before. But, on the other hand, it isn't surprising that somebody raised in Beirut would have strong feelings on such matters. And Shira needs to react the way she imagines an American might.

"I do believe there are innocent people in the world who shouldn't be killed for things others do."

"Easy for you to say," Raya responds. "You're protected on all sides by oceans, or friendly neighbors. You're safe. That must be nice."

Shira smiles at the incongruity of the statement. She's tempted to disclose who she really is and have a legitimate conversation about who's safe and who isn't.

But, of course, that would be foolish.

"You're right, of course," she finally answers. "I can't even imagine the life you have to live. Nor can anybody else in the United States. We are a lucky people. Celebrating our Bicentennial as we speak, by the way."

Shira has saved up that little tidbit for just the right moment. To authenticate her cover, and to take the edge off.

But it doesn't matter. Raya could care less about some American holiday, and she isn't done venting yet.

"Your economy is strong. You have the most powerful military in the world. You live a life so safe, and so easy, that you can't really identify with what we suffer through every day."

Again, Shira agrees, although she imagines there are plenty of Americans who might argue that their life isn't that safe or easy.

Raya goes on, "And you feel you shouldn't be touched because you're so innocent? It's your government that starts wars and kills people, not you. Right?"

Shira sees no reason to defend Americans just because she's pretending to be one. On the other hand, although much of what Raya is saying makes some sense, Shira actually does believe that innocent people shouldn't die just because of what their government does. That's what terrorists believe, and one of the reasons why Shira is fighting them.

"So, what are we going to do today?" she asks, changing the subject to something less controversial, a tactic which seems to work. They don't talk about what happened at Entebbe for the rest of the day.

The next morning Shira is up early, and decides to have breakfast with Majed, something she rarely does. Their relationship has become much more cordial since the frank conversation of a few days ago, and she wants to capitalize on every opportunity to gather intel from him.

"Sleep well?" she asks him, while looking in the refrigerator for something to eat.

"Yes. All things considered. The eggs are in the bottom drawer, by the way."

"Want one?" she asks.

"No. Got to go. Early meeting."

"Would you consider bringing me into the office some day?" Shira asks, having decided she needs to be a little more aggressive if she's going to get any official intel. It's certainly not going to come from dinner conversations.

"Why would I do that?" he answers.

"Because I'm fun to have around and can be helpful doing things nobody else wants to do."

"Like what?"

"Like finding your lost President," Shira jokes.

Majed laughs and says, "For a minute there I thought you were serious."

"I am," she answers softly, but Majed has already left.

Later that morning, with nothing better to do, Shira decides to walk over to American University and audit a class. She usually sits in on a language or political science class but today she has opted for a lecture called "What drives Muslims to terror?" a subject that certainly interests her, both personally and professionally.

Shira has several reasons for going to school when she has the opportunity. One, it bolsters her story that she's here as a transfer student. Two, she's actually learning things that can help her in her budding career. And three, it keeps her from going stark raving mad since, once she completes and files her daily report, the rest of the day she has very little to do. Raya goes to summer classes. Zaina does her daily errands. And Majed is working unusually long hours, as he helps break in the new administration. So, nobody is around to provide social stimulation of any kind.

Which, given Shira's risky undercover role, is probably a good thing.

Today Shira decides to walk to class, not only because it takes up time, but it helps her understand Beirut better. Everywhere there are remnants of what must have been an incredibly vibrant life. Apartment houses that probably had doormen at one time. Buildings' pock-marked by bomb and bullet holes. Parks that are now overgrown with weeds and covered with rubbish. Wide avenues that hint of traffic, now long gone, and of people who must have strolled these sidewalks, looking in store windows, in search of something beautiful, and expensive, to buy.

War kills people, Shira thinks as she walks. *But it can just as effectively kill a city. As it has Beirut. This was known as the Paris of the Middle East. It was a wealthy city, a gathering spot for students, artists, writers, and many of the most cultured people in the world. There was a highly educated leisure class, who frequented the now shuttered coffee shops, restaurants, and bars, discussing weighty things that mattered then, such as books, art, politics, and the meaning of life. Beirut had a soul back then.*

As Shira looks around the city now, she can barely imagine that other Beirut. The evidences of war are everywhere; the rubble, the craters, even the soldiers wandering about here and there. And above all, the squalor of a city nobody cares about anymore.

This is now a boring and angry city, she thinks. *There are few people around. No casual conversations. No nods of greeting. And above all, no humor. Danger normally breeds a special kind of dark humor. Like in Ireland during their "troubles." Or Czechoslovakia during its two occupations. And especially in Israel.*

But I see none of that here in Beirut.

Perhaps, Shira surmises, *in order for people to laugh together, there must be shared friends, common experiences, and well-identified enemies. But everything in Beirut is so random and uncontrolled. What can these people laugh about? And with whom?*

Once seated in the back row of a classroom, and waiting for the instructor, Shira continues to wonder why anybody would knowingly take something so vitally alive as the Paris of the Middle East, and destroy it. Squeeze the life out of it, in fact.

And for what? Unfortunately, nothing she learns in the classroom helps her answer that question.

Once Shira is back in the still empty Kahn house, she calls Ari and confirms that, as Raya suspected, the Israeli government considers their Entebbe raid an unqualified success.

Surprisingly, he says, the Mossad role in the operation isn't common knowledge yet, in Israel or elsewhere. But it will be, of course.

People have questions about how the Israeli military was able to strike so surgically, and to limit the casualties so effectively. And about who was the mastermind behind the attack? Netanyahu led it but who developed the plan? Based on what information?

But nobody knows the extent of the undercover work that was done before the raid, Ari tells her, nor the role of the French pilot's wife who provided the Israeli soldiers with such valuable pre-raid intel.

"That's too bad," he laments.

But Shira is happy that her role is hidden. At least for now. It isn't good for an undercover agent to get too well-known outside the circles that really matter.

****

"Majed, look at this crazy request," Shira says to her boss as he passes by her desk.

"They want us to bulldoze the buildings over on Rue Gouraud. The same ones that were bombed just yesterday."

"Has the bomb squad cleared the site yet?" Majed asks.

"That's the point exactly. No, they haven't. It's still an active combat zone and deemed unsafe for bomb crews to go in and sanitize things. But these idiots think we should send construction workers in, anyway."

"All of Beirut is an active combat zone. If we wait until it's truly safe, we'll get no work done at all," Majed responds. "See if the crew finishing up on Harma Street can get over there right away."

He turns away to address another logistical issue, and Shira is shocked by the casualness of it all. The site is deemed too risky for soldiers. But these innocent and unarmed workers are asked to just put on their hard hats and go to work as if it were a pothole in Paris or London that needs repairing. To her, it's crazy.

But she does as she's told.

It's only been a few weeks since Shira started working with Majed, but already she's been a big help to the Ministers and a godsend to the clerical staff.

The chaos and inefficiency she found was truly mind-boggling. The clerk assigned to Majed and his department was overwhelmed from the get-go, and kept jumping from one unfinished task to another as she tried to meet the needs of the overly-demanding Ministers around her.

In the beginning Shira just followed her around, finishing up whatever the clerk started. Getting files back where they belonged or arranging for previously typed job orders to be signed and sent.

That was all helpful, of course, but highly inefficient. Now, in the interest of saving time, Shira has diplomatically inserted herself earlier in the process where she can actually eliminate duplication, consolidate job orders, and circumvent red tape.

She does all of this so easily and efficiently that, in a short time, she's become almost indispensable to Majed, and to the rest of the Ministers who share the office as well. The once overwhelmed clerk now effectively reports to Shira, as do several others. They all happily do the menial tasks she assigns without ever questioning her authority to give orders.

Why? Because she has Majed's confidence, of course, but, more importantly, she knows what she's doing.

Without any formal notification to the staff, or any training, Shira has slipped into the role of Majed's "right hand man" as easily as she did the role of a pilot's wife. It's what she does.

"Fatima, where did you put the job order authorizing red crew two to begin their work?" Shira shouts above the noise. "We need to get a copy posted at the job site."

"It's in the top drawer, Peggy," Fatima answers. "I'll get it. How many copies do you need?"

"Two," she says aloud, then thinks to herself, *I need one for the job site, one for the file, and one for Ari?*

"Make that three," she says, without much thought to the danger of leaving a paper trail that a suspicious government worker could follow.

Thankfully, everything is too disorganized to worry about that.

Back in Tel Aviv, there is now a staff of three clerks at Mossad headquarters whose full-time job is to read, analyze, and process the volumes of paperwork being generated by their highly productive spy in Beirut.

Every morning several manilla folders of information arrive by mail, some with messages describing what is in the folders but most with no instructions at all, requiring sorting and prioritization before they are distributed to the appropriate agents. And occasionally to the Prime Minister himself.

Yitzhak Hofi believes that a major responsibility of his is to keep Menachem Begin personally apprised of events in the agency, and by extension, the effectiveness of their field agents. It turns out that Begin is a curious man, who doesn't just listen to what Hofi says. He interrupts often and

116

asks about details that aren't in the written reports. For instance, during a discussion about their strategy in Lebanon, Begin asks about the reliability of the information.

"Can we trust the intel we are using to make this decision?" Begin asks. "Is it primary or secondary?"

"Very much primary. Our source is a young female agent who is living with the family of one of the Ministers, and occasionally even helps him out at his office. She's become one of our most valuable assets."

"A female?" Begin asks. "In Beirut? Unescorted?"

"What do you mean?"

"Shouldn't we have one of our male spies there in Lebanon to watch out for her. Just in case."

"You don't know Shira, sir," Hofi answers, smiling, "she prefers to operate alone, and I have to say she's been very effective so far. Besides, if we need every female operative to be escorted, why employ any females at all?"

"Good question."

"Believe me, there are situations where a female spy is far more effective than a male would be," Hofi goes on, "and, so far, at least, Shira has proven that point in spades. She's become one of our most valuable assets."

"Is she attractive?"

"Yes, as a matter of fact, she is. Why do you ask?"

"Doesn't that work against the whole idea of somebody working undercover? Won't she be noticed?"

"First of all, sir, with a little effort you can make an attractive asset look ordinary but not the other way around," Hofi says, stating an incontrovertible fact. "And you must know, sir," he goes on, "that there are situations where an attractive woman can accomplish things an ordinary woman can't."

"I see," the Prime Minister says turning away, just the hint of a smile touching his face. Then, as he turns back toward his spymaster, the smile disappears quickly, making Hofi wonder if it was there at all.

And the two men go on to weightier matters.

****

Much of the intel Shira is sending back to Tel Aviv now relates to the escalating violence in the southern part of Lebanon. There are major skirmishes developing between the Israeli Army and its archenemy, the PLO, with southern Lebanon serving as the battleground.

Because it doesn't fall under his purview, Majed is not directly involved in dealing with the PLO or any of the other organizations using Lebanon as a staging ground for their attacks on Israel. But he is often around the Prime Minister or his staff when these matters are discussed and debated. So, although much of what Shira is passing on comes second-hand to her, it's like gold to her handlers.

And, because Majed is so frustrated with the situation, he isn't as cautious as normal. Often, late in the evening, after their mostly clerical work is finished, he calls Shira into his office to vent. And that's when she gets some of her most valuable nuggets.

Of course, what he says is unsubstantiated and unverifiable, which she notes assiduously, but it also is the most highly read of anything she submits. Majed would be shocked at how much his rants are educating the Israeli government, and affecting their decision making.

As reported, Elias Sarkis has finally been installed as the legitimately elected Prime Minister of Lebanon but his political position is still very weak. So weak, in fact, that the PLO operates independently and never discusses anything with him or his government.

Which frustrates Majed no end. His government is toothless, and seemingly OK with it.

The PLO has now established a quasi-state in southern Lebanon, reporting to no one, which they have used as a base operation for raids into northern Israel for months, if not years. They have no interest in discussing their strategies with anybody, especially Lebanon, whose objectives, in the final analysis, may not be totally aligned with theirs anyway.

So far, the Israel response has been largely proportional, as they have simply conducted their own raids into Lebanese territory, sometimes leveling entire Palestinian towns, but more often hitting camps that they perceive to be PLO-controlled. But the problem is that their tit-for-tat strategy isn't changing the dynamics on the ground much.

Shira has made it clear in her reports that the Lebanese government is not functioning well, and that no rational decisions can be expected from its leadership in the short-term. Certainly, Lebanon doesn't have the backbone to join the PLO in its fight.

So, Israel decides the time is right to get more aggressive.

"Everything has escalated in the last few days. Israel is now even bombing us," Majed says in response to a pointed question from Shira. "Those bastards are killing our people."

"Are you sure that it isn't just more of the same, Israel retaliating for the PLO attacks?" Shira asks.

"That's not what I'm hearing. Sarkis considers their latest provocations an act of war. Requiring some kind of response. Got to go to an emergency cabinet meeting. Talk to you later."

And just like that, Shira finds herself in a dangerous front-line position of what could be a burgeoning war between her native country and the one she is spying on.

Not the safest place to be.

****

Shira hears about it first from Raya.

"I wanted to talk to you before anybody else did," Raya says. "An American tourist was killed in Israel, by a group of terrorists, called Fatah, who were led by a young girl from our country."

"What?"

"It's all over the news. Evidently, they crossed the border, killed the woman, then, hijacked a bus."

"Why?"

"Who knows why terrorists do these sorts of things?" Raya answers. "Religion? Hate? They don't know any better? But I'm sorry about what I said about you Americans the other day. I feel like, in some strange way, I caused this."

"Have they been captured?" Shira asks, ignoring Raya's attempt to make amends.

"Not yet. They hijacked the bus near Haifa and were headed toward Tel Aviv. They may have even switched to another bus, taken some hostages."

"Why do people do these things?" Shira asks again rhetorically.

"Only Allah knows."

Shira's mind is racing a mile a minute. Naturally her first thoughts are professional. *What can I do to help my country? How can I find out about the involvement of the Lebanese government? Figure out what they may do? And get a report to Ari as soon as possible.*

"Where is Majed?" she asks.

"He left to go to his office," Raya replies. "I suppose there will be a cabinet meeting to discuss what the official response should be. Why do you ask?"

"I need to get to him," Shira says.

"Good God, why?" is Raya's response.

The question is an appropriate one. Raya wonders why 'Peggy' is running toward the problem instead of away from it. If terrorists are going after Americans, she should be trying to get on the first plane out.

So, Shira tries to explain, "I need to talk to Majed. He'll know what I should do. I just can't deal with this on my own."

Then, she starts to cry. Big, dramatic goblets of tears, as only a distraught girl, or a talented actress, could produce. The show is convincing. Raya agrees to drive her to the office.

Once there, Shira does a search of all the messages or telexes that have been received in the last few hours. Nothing on the developing crisis, which is probably not surprising since her department has little "need to know" at this point. Then she leaves the office to find Majed but encounters a colleague along the way.

"Any news on the American that was killed?" she asks.

"Yes. The attackers were from the Fatah branch of the PLO, and they escaped by commandeering a bus. Then, while being chased, they went on a bloody rampage. As I understand it, over 100 Israelis have been killed or wounded so far."

"Oh, no," Shira gasps. "Have they been stopped yet?"

"Don't know. But it puts us in the crosshairs. We're sure that Israel will respond," the colleague went on, "We just don't know how, or when. Our military is on high alert and civilians are being warned to stay at home."

"Why would Israel attack Beirut if it was the PLO behind the bus hijacking?" Shira asks.

"It isn't that simple. They accuse us of harboring the PLO even though we have literally no control over them. Kind of hard to draw clear lines of responsibility in this damned war. Gotta go. I've got a lot to do."

Shira decides that her priority has now changed. She needs to reach Ari rather than Majed. What the Lebanese government might do is suddenly less significant than what her own government might do.

"Where the hell have you been?" Ari says as he picks up the phone. "We've been worried sick."

"I've—"

"Never mind. Just get to the airport right away."

"Don't you need me to stay? Be your agent behind enemy lines?" Shira asks. "I can learn a lot in the next few hours."

"No. Just get to the airport right away and call me from there. I'll have your extraction arranged as quickly as I can," Ari says. "And don't stay in those Beirut government offices any longer than you have to. I'm not privy to what our military is planning but it could be almost anything at this point."

"I need to tell Majed and Raya I'm leaving."

"Absolutely not. This is no time for courtesies. Your assignment is over. You'll never see those people again."

"That sounds ominous."

"Do I have to spell it out for you, Shira," Ari is yelling now. "The situation is extremely volatile and you're in danger from all sides. At the moment, you have no friends except me. So, get the hell out of there."

Which Shira does.

Chapter 11
Tel Aviv

Surprisingly, when she gets home, Shira finds her apartment has been freshened up for her arrival.

There are newly purchased groceries in the cupboard, colorful flowers on the coffee table, an ice bucket containing a bottle of champagne in the living room, and propped up on her desk in plain sight is a light blue envelope.

Half expecting it to be from Aaron, she quickly opens it and reads the note inside.

"Welcome home. Nice job in Beirut. Enjoy the bubbly, and I'll be in touch, Ari."

Shira's disappointed. Now that Aaron knows where she lives, she secretly hoped it would be from him, not her boss. It's nice to be appreciated but far better to be loved.

It's crazy, she knows, but with everything she's had to focus on these last few months, playing a variety of undercover roles, in exotic settings, she's found herself thinking more and more about Aaron.

I want some stability, she thinks. *Somebody to come home to, and talk to, and above all, somebody who'll tell me everything will be OK. Whether it's true or not.*

Shira knows in her heart that it isn't a good thing to be thinking that way. Her job has many positives, not the least of which is excitement. But the biggest negative is that it's impossible to have a normal relationship.

Back at the beginning, when she could just take or leave Aaron on her own terms, things worked just fine. But loving him and fitting him into her chaotic life on a regular basis? And building something of substance on a foundation of lies? She knows that won't work long-term. So, for now a romance with Aaron has to be on the back-burner.

Ari has prescribed rest and relaxation. Unfortunately, Shira's not that type of girl. She doesn't just rest, ever. And relax? Forget it. She doesn't even read for pleasure.

To her, real life is much more interesting than fiction. She doesn't like to watch television. She has no hobbies and prefers short bursts of exercise rather than casual runs, or long bike rides. And, above all, Shira hates the tourist things.

Far too boring, she thinks. *Why visit a church or museum just to relive the past, when there's so much going on in the present? Or sit at a coffee shop and idly watch life, and people, pass me by. While I do nothing.*

Shira is addicted to action. So, the first morning of her sabbatical, with nothing else to do, she calls Ari, just to chat about what's going on.

She finds out that, indeed, an invasion of southern Lebanon is imminent. She also finds out that her undercover work at the Entebbe Airport is now common knowledge within the agency, although the official story is that they got their intel from blueprints and flyovers rather than an informant.

In fact, Ninette Morenu isn't even mentioned in internal documents, nor has her name surfaced in Israeli newspapers. But, more importantly and thankfully, neither has Shira's name. She's still unknown to the general public. Inside Mossad, though, Shira is a hot commodity. Now that she's back, everybody wants her on their assignments.

"We should use Shira on this one," is a common refrain but, like a talent agent, Ari has been protecting his asset from overexposure, saving her only for the most important of jobs. What has become obvious to him, though, is that, given the demand, he needs another Shira.

So, once again, Ari is scouring student lists and school directories, looking for females with attributes similar to Shira.

She needs to be attractive, which can be disarming to male targets. She needs to be smart, able to think on her feet. And especially, she needs to be creative because there hasn't been an operation yet that goes according to plan.

An asset that can't improvise often ends up dead.

But, above all, his new recruit needs to be loyal and patriotic. Somebody who won't question her assignments, no matter how inappropriate or immoral they may seem.

All of this is unknown to Shira, of course. She still thinks of herself as a neophyte agent, not a model for other recruits.

In fact, if she knew that Ari was looking to clone her already, she might strenuously object, which is exactly why Ari hasn't told her of his intentions.

****

Partway through her forced sabbatical, Shira gets a call from Eliana.

"You free for lunch," the secretary asks. "I'd love to catch up on things."

Shira is thrilled to hear from Eliana. She no longer considers her just a business colleague. More like a friend. And she can really use some sympathetic female companionship right about now.

They meet at Raphael's, a chic Mediterranean-style restaurant near the office that is frequented by Mossad personnel. So, just to be safe, they ask for a table at the back of the restaurant where they won't be overheard.

The first few minutes, over drinks, the two share office gossip, much like any women who work in an office might. Who's being transferred and where. Who's seeing whom. Who's getting divorced. Stuff like that.

Except the gossip in a spy organization like Mossad is a little more guarded, because some of the juicier details have to be muted, or even left out, to protect the confidential nature of what they do.

As an example, Elena reveals that Caleb is seeing Rachel but she doubts the romance has legs.

"Why's that?" Shira asks.

"He'll be shipping out on assignment soon."

"Where's he going?"

"Not allowed to say."

"When will he get back?"

"That's confidential too. But probably not soon enough to keep Rachel from finding another lover."

"So, it'll be more than twenty-four hours."

"Exactly."

Then, well into the conversation, Eliana asks, "Speaking of lovers, how's your old boyfriend, Aaron. Has he been around lately?"

"Ari told me not to see him again. Remember?" Shira replies cautiously, a smile on her face.

"Of course, I remember. But you're dodging the question."

"Well, I tried to obey Ari, I really did. But Aaron wouldn't cooperate," Shira replies. "He can be persistent at times."

"Not surprising," Eliana replies. "Especially since I doubt you dissuaded him much. So, you've been seeing him?"

"Not seeing him exactly, Eliana," Shira answers. "Remember. I've been on assignment in Beirut."

"OK, let me rephrase the question, counselor," Eliana says with a smile on her face. "Have you been with Aaron since Ari told you to break it up? Yes or no?"

"Well, when you phrase it that way, the answer is yes."

"Remember, Shira," Eliana cautions. "Ari thinks Aaron can't be trusted. You're playing with fire here."

"Believe me, I haven't told Aaron anything about anything," Shira counters. "And, as to his trustworthiness, I think Ari is full of shit," Shira asserts. "There's no more honest, or patriotic, guy on the planet than Aaron."

"Ari has some kind of evidence that proves otherwise. At least that's what he's told me," Eliana argues.

"Screw his evidence," Shira replies, her face turning red. "I know Aaron better than Ari does. And the guy couldn't lie if he had to. Everything he thinks or feels is written indelibly on his face."

"I'll bet he says the same about you. And look how wrong he is on that. Anyway, you sound like a woman in love."

"I'm not sure about that," Shira argues. "Obviously, I'm attracted to the guy. But I would never tell Aaron anything. Not what I do. Or who I work for. And certainly not anything about the Mossad, or its operations."

"I believe that, Shira," Eliana says. "And I assure you that, as I promised in the beginning, I won't tell Ari about our conversation either. But be careful, girl. If Aaron isn't squeaky clean, he could ruin your reputation here."

"Look. I haven't heard from Aaron in weeks. I'm not sure we have a relationship at this point. And, as a brand new agent, I doubt I have much of a reputation to protect anyway."

"On that, my dear Shira, I think you'd be very much surprised."

****

Since returning from her forced vacation, Shira has been busy doing clerical work and odd jobs in support of other teams. Nothing as exotic as what she did in Uganda and Beirut, but valuable to Mossad anyway. And her skills have caught the attention of others in the organization.

On occasion, in the hall or cafeteria, somebody comes up to introduce themselves and compliment her work. But most don't have the courage to do that. They just point her out to others and talk behind her back.

One, however, has the guts to call her and try to recruit her away.

"Miss Adelson," the voice on the phone begins. "We've never met but my name is Gabriel Hoffman. I'm a handler like your boss, Ari Lavon, and I work with agents stationed in Syria and Egypt. I've been watching your work from afar and I must say that I'm very impressed."

"Thank you," she says. "But I'm embarrassed to say that I've never heard of you. Where do you work exactly?"

"I have an office on the third floor but I'm hardly ever there," he replies. "I work out of Damascus or Cairo. Hotel rooms mostly."

"OK, Mr. Hoffman. What can I do for you?"

"Well, I'm in town for a few days and wondered if we might grab a cup of coffee?"

"To talk about?" Shira asks.

"Let's save that for when we get together," he answers. "Oh, and for the time being, I'd appreciate it if you don't tell Ari I contacted you. He can be so territorial."

"I won't, but I don't know if I can meet you. I'm pretty busy," Shira explains.

"How about I meet you in the company cafeteria in five minutes. I won't take more than a half-hour of your time."

What could be safer than the Mossad cafeteria? She thinks, *And I'm curious to find out what this guy wants.*

So, against her better judgement, she says yes.

When she walks into the cafeteria, a tall, dark-haired, forty-something guy stands up and waves at her. He's well-dressed, confident, and good looking.

Here we go, she thinks, *Finally, the kind of spy I've been looking for since I got here. Like in the movies.*

After taking care of the introductions and niceties, Gabriel gets right down to business.

"I have an offer to make," he begins. "I'd like you to join my team, in sort of the same role you've been performing for Ari. But, because we have a lot going on in my sector, I'd keep you much busier. You would be out on assignment most of the time, but when you're not, your time is your own, to do with what you want. I won't make you hang around here doing meaningless work that's, frankly, beneath you."

Shira is taken aback. It never entered her mind that handlers might compete for assets. She assumed that, since Ari had recruited her and trained her, he would be her boss until she got promoted or transferred.

"I'm here because I'm still training. Ari wants me to know how important the support roles are."

"But they're not. Mossad is all about its agents. And a good handler keeps them busy, not sitting at a desk writing reports."

"I'm not sure I agree with that," Shira argues. "I'd feel pretty alone out there without somebody back here interacting with me, and helping."

"That's the thing," Gabriel goes on. "I'm more 'hands on' than Ari. I'll either be part of every operation you do, or very close by, just in case. As you know, Ari is kind of old-school, sitting behind a desk, moving his agents around out in the field, without getting his hands dirty. But, with me, we're more like a team. You would have my support."

Given how handsome Gabriel is, she tells herself, *I might like his support, and even be OK with a 'hands-on' approach. But I have reservations about his offer. First of all, I don't like him going behind Ari's back. I'm sure it's against protocol, and I'm surprised a guy so young would be 'ballsy' enough to try it with Ari. Secondly, and more importantly, I feel a loyalty toward Ari that I hadn't thought about before. But it's there.*

Gabriel senses her reluctance, leans forward in a conspiratorial manner, and talks in a whisper, forcing Shira to do the same.

"Let me be frank," Gabriel whispers. "You're riding the wrong horse here. Ari has outlived his usefulness. Don't get me wrong. I love the guy. But he's no longer a superstar."

"And you are?"

Gabriel looks in her eyes for a few seconds and begins to smile in a way that answers her question immodestly without saying a word.

"Let me just say this. We're in two different stages of our careers, Ari and me. You being tied to him doesn't make any sense, given that you're on the rise, and he isn't. We would be a far better fit." Then, he winks.

Shira doesn't know Gabriel at all but, already, she doesn't like him. *Looks can only go so far,* she thinks, *until, like cheap wallpaper covering a bad wall, the flaws begin to show through.*

At least Ari is straight-forward and honest. And, when he makes a decision, he has her best interest in mind. He talks to her regularly. He keeps her informed. And, best of all, he trusts her to do her job.

Gabriel may be right about Ari being old-school but he's wrong about Shira. Turns out she's old-school too.

"I've decided to cut you a break," she says to Gabriel, leaning in as he did before. "I'm not going to tell Ari we had this conversation—as long as you never call me again. Have a nice day."

****

At times, Shira regrets her decision.

The last few months have been very boring. Ari hasn't been able to give her assignments commensurate with her talents. So, even though she does what she's told, as competently as possible, her mind is elsewhere.

It's natural. She's a healthy young woman with time on her hands and no "somebody special" to share it with.

She's been on a few dates, mostly suggestions from girls in the office, but none that meet her expectations. One guy was her intellectual equal but absolutely too nerdy to take seriously. Another had the kind of looks she likes but lacked depth. And the third was just pathetic in every way.

One thing is abundantly clear to Shira. There isn't an Aaron among them, and then, unexpectedly, he calls.

"Nice exit," Aaron says, as if she had snuck out on him days ago, rather than weeks.

"My specialty."

"Are you still gone, or can we get together?" he asks.

"I'd like that," she answers, secretly thrilled that Aaron is finding his way back into her life again. And just like that, their sporadic, but truly special, love affair is on again.

They have dinner at a restaurant the first night, see a play the second, and go dancing the third. But all three dates end up the same. Either back at her place, or his, for a full night of lovemaking.

For months Shira's been feeling like a celibate nun. Now, she's making up for lost time.

At some point, Shira tells herself, *I need to strike a happy balance. But this isn't the time for that. Not with Aaron finally back in my life.*

Occasionally, Shira worries about the uncomfortable fact that Ari ordered her to stop seeing Aaron. However, at the time, she was a raw recruit trying to impress her boss. And she couldn't imagine disobeying him.

But, now, she has the credentials to do whatever she wants. And, seeing Aaron again is what she wants, no matter what Ari thinks. She won't tell him she's violated his order, of course, but if he ever asks, she'll be honest, but steadfast.

Aaron is her soulmate, and she'll never be convinced he's a threat of any kind. Most importantly though, Aaron fills a hole in her soul that has been there since Shira decided to cut ties with her family. In a way, he is family, and their old relationship is blossoming again.

They're dating like they did in college, exploring Tel Aviv, the city they both love, as if it was their first time there. They're together every weekend, visiting galleries, museums, and flea markets, things Shira never would think of doing alone. And they're going to plays, catching movies they may have missed, or just walking around the old city of Jaffa, enjoying each other's company as much as the scenery. Just like the old days.

Their favorite place to hang out is Yarkon Park. Most weekends they find themselves there, reading, playing cards, or even enjoying board games, watching the people, and talking. Mostly talking.

Often, their discussions spill over into the early evenings, over cocktails or dinner. They have many common interests but they make it a point to keep things as light-hearted as possible, avoiding anything controversial. In fact, there's a kind of unspoken pact. Aaron won't talk about his efforts to find common ground with their Arab adversaries. And Shira won't talk about what she's actually doing to undermine those very same efforts.

Aaron still doesn't know what Shira does for a living. She once said she was selling feminine products, which he figures is a lie. She's talked about shuffling papers as if she's a secretary or stenographer. Which is hardly Shira's skill set. And, then, she disappears for days or weeks. Always vague about where or when.

Any time the conversation gets uncomfortably close to what she does, Shira clams up. And Aaron has learned that, if he asks too many questions, she cuts the evening off quickly, without so much as a "good night" kiss. So, he doesn't do that anymore.

Mostly they talk about books they've read, plays they want to see, people they admire, and occasionally they dip their toes into Israeli politics, but only for brief conversations on people and policies. Never issues.

Until, one evening when, over drinks, the conversation goes a little deeper. They begin to discuss the peace efforts that concluded that spring with the highly-touted Egyptian-Israeli Peace Treaty.

They weren't dating each other at the time but, in retrospect, they found that they shared the same interests and optimism back then.

The U.S. President Jimmy Carter, risking considerable time and political capital, decided to wade into the stalemated Arab-Israeli peace talks. Something they both agreed was sorely needed.

He held a summit at Camp David, his summer retreat, that lasted two weeks and although it started out well, with all parties actively participating, it quickly deteriorated into a series of one-on-one meetings with the two combative delegations from Israel and Egypt both holding firm on demands that seemed impossible for the other to meet.

Still, afterward, the persistent Mr. Carter, with Egyptian President Sadat's consent, traveled to Israel and over three days, hammered out an historic Egyptian-Israeli Treaty that was finalized on March 26, 1979, with the blessing of both countries. It was an incredible event, highly celebrated by most Israelis. Less so by the Arabs. Still, the prospects for peace had never burned brighter than they did at that moment.

But, now, here on a park bench in Tel Aviv, both Shira and Aaron feel that the promise of that incredible, precedent setting event has been squandered.

They just disagree about who was at fault.

"Carter needed to stay personally involved," Aaron argues, "making a treaty is one thing. An important thing, of course. But making it work is another. It's so typical of the U.S. to meddle for a few months and then, go away."

Shira notices Aaron is getting angry. But so is she. And she can't help herself from wading in with her own questions, and opinions.

"When do we take responsibility for our own affairs, Aaron?" Shira counters. "We can't always blame the Americans for everything."

"Not always, but in this case we certainly can," he responds in a voice louder than it needs to be. "Listen, Shira, this is something I know a little bit about. You should listen to me for a change."

Shira isn't sure what he means by that, or why this debate is escalating into a fight, but it doesn't stop her from continuing to express her opinion, loudly and vociferously.

"I know a little about these things, too. There's a time for talking and a time for doing," she says. "Carter did the talking. He got a deal. Now it's up to us to enforce it."

"What do you mean enforce it?" he asks. "Any negotiation requires people on both sides willing to give a little. But that can't happen without a fair, unbiased arbitrator in the middle of it, keeping things moving. Somebody has to build trust between the two parties. Carter did that. But he didn't follow up as he should have."

"The United States did what they could," Shira says. "Now, we have to move forward on our own. The treaty's done. Our job is to make it work in the real world."

"Your real world?" Aaron asks. "Or mine?"

"What do you mean by that?"

"You're not really about making things work, now, are you, Shira? You're more about breaking them. And punishing people who won't cooperate."

"You have no idea what I'm about," Shira says in a voice growing louder by the minute as she tries to match his intensity. "I want peace as much as you do."

"You have a funny way of showing it," Aaron shouts as he gets up from the park bench. "Give me a call when you're ready to talk about what you do for a living, as an example. And, more importantly why you do it."

"I'll do that."

"Then, maybe I'll do the same."

****

For months now, Ari has been talking to female candidates about joining the agency. He's had little trouble finding attractive ones, or smart ones, or ones with a strong personality.

But finding all of those characteristics in one person? Not so easy.

How rare a find Shira was is becoming abundantly clear. To Ari, yes. But also to everybody else in the agency. As a result, he's getting pressure to put her back into the field, both from his boss and from Shira herself. So, he's done that, in a few minor operations, always in a support role.

Like surveillance, which she excels at.

Not only is she able to disguise herself in a way that makes her invisible, but her patience and attention-to-detail are both off-the-charts. On one operation, for instance, she was assigned the responsibility of keeping tabs on a target, all by herself, which she does for several days. With almost no time to sleep. When the target turns on his light to read a book at 2:12 a.m. on the second night of surveillance, it is duly noted in her log. His 4:24 a.m. snack on the third night is entered as well. And on the fifth night, when he surprisingly slips out of his apartment at 5:37 a.m., wearing a black hooded sweatshirt to conceal his identity, she isn't fooled a bit.

And, as he speeds out of the parking garage on his motorcycle, she is right behind him, on a motorcycle that she had rented, just in case she needed it.

On another operation, she convinces a young male night clerk at a hotel that she is a poor college student desperately in need of some shuteye. So, he allows her to spend the night sleeping on a couch off the lobby, where she has an unobstructed view of anybody going to and from the elevator bank. Which allows her to see the target when he tries to sneak out in the middle of the night.

All of these assignments help in Shira's development. But mainly, they keep her occupied while Ari searches for her next major operation. He can afford to be picky. In Shira, he has a valuable asset, maybe the most valuable ever, and he intends to use her in a way that can help her, the agency, and him.

Coincidentally, they are both sitting in Ari's office when the right opportunity surfaces. A call comes in from a couple of agents, who are on assignment in Paris. They feel that, if she can be in Paris by the next night, Shira could play an important role in their operation.

"Our target likes to drink and socialize with women," one of the agents, a guy named Leon Cohen, tells Ari. "As guys, we can watch him, of course, and look for the right opportunity to connect with him. But, honestly, with Shira, he'll be far less guarded, and she'll have more opportunities to engage."

"Sounds dangerous," Ari replies. "What do you mean engage?"

"Come on, Ari, you know what I mean. Flirt. Do the whole seduction thing. Get him loose-lipped."

Ari covers the mouthpiece and says to Shira, "Would you wait outside for a minute. Don't go anywhere because I may have an assignment for you."

After she leaves, Ari gets back on the phone and says to the agent, "Listen, Leon, Shira is relatively new to the agency. She hasn't been asked to "engage" before and I need to know exactly how you intend to use her."

Ari hears some muffled discussion over the phone and then some laughing. Then, Leon returns to the phone.

"Listen Ari. You know as well as I do that we don't know what will happen on an operation like this. We've been told that your girl is attractive, speaks French fluently, is adept at playing roles, and can be seductive if asked. Is that true?"

"Yes, but she's young and inexperienced," Ari replies. "I wouldn't like her to be alone with an amorous, inebriated older man at this stage of her career, no matter how important the guy is to us."

"Are you waiting until she's old and unattractive?"

"Just until she's a little more experienced."

"Frankly, I'm guessing she's way more experienced than you think she is," the agent says. "But here's what we'll do. If we think she's being put into a compromising position, we'll give you a call before doing it, OK?"

"Who's the target?" Ari answers, avoiding the question entirely.

"Yahia el-Mashad," he replies, "the Egyptian scientist that heads up Iran's nuclear program."

****

As excited as Ari is about finding Shira an operation to work on, he's equally excited about finding a new female candidate that he thinks might work out well for Mossad.

She's not quite as attractive as Shira, nor does she have the same kind of experience. But, she's even more aggressive, maybe even smarter, and has an outgoing personality that can take over a room at times.

So, she should be able to handle the macho culture of the agency, an important consideration. She's not one to back down from a fight, no matter what the personality, gender, or power of her adversary.

Obviously, Ari tells himself, *one of my problems will be controlling her. She's cocky and headstrong, which are good traits in an agent, but hard to manage. Fortunately,*

I've had some experience with Shira. And the secret is to show no weakness, and never back down.

Her name is Miriam Schwartz and she comes from a well-established family in Tel Aviv. She's been working on her PHD in Humanities but has come to realize that, after school, she most likely will be teaching at some college. Which doesn't sound very exciting to her. And working with the Mossad, being an undercover agent, with all its excitement and danger, does.

"How soon will I get into the field?" she asks Ari.

"Maybe never," he replies, "if you don't take your training more seriously and learn how to take orders."

"Not my strong suit. I'm kind of an improviser."

"You're kind of a pain in the ass, Miriam," Ari responds. "That's what you are. You should know that all great agents know how to take orders and color inside the lines if they have to. It's an important skill set.

"I want to go undercover, be a spy, pretend to be somebody I'm not," Miriam argues. "That's what appeals to me."

"OK. Then, how about this. You pretend to be somebody who takes orders," Ari says. "And when you've perfected that role maybe we'll put you out in the field."

"Very funny," she replies.

Ari goes back to his paperwork, signaling that Miriam has been dismissed.

She gets up to leave, not noticing the tiny grin creeping onto Ari's face. The more he interacts with Miriam, the more confident he is that she will be every bit as effective as Shira has been, thereby doubling his capability to support operations that could use a female agent.

Still, there's so much left for Miriam to learn.

Ari learned with Shira that he needs to sprinkle in some action with the initial training, or any potential agent worth their salt, and especially one like Miriam will get bored.

But he can't just send her out on an operation without any idea who the enemy really is and/or how to react when challenged.

It was hard enough to teach Shira how to play a submissive female when necessary. With Miriam's personality it may be next to impossible. Only time, and experience, will tell.

Ari does know, however, that, like Shira, at some point Miriam has to find out how to operate in the field alone, and he can only do so much to get her ready.

But that doesn't mean he won't worry, as he is right now with Shira on her way to Paris to engage with Yahia El-Mashad in what could be her dangerous operation yet.

Chapter 12
Paris

"Why can't I do it," Shira asks Leon Cohen at their first meeting in Paris. "I can get into the guy's room as easily as anybody."

"Ari forbid it," agent Cohen replies. "Evidently, you're too precious to put on the front lines in a perilous situation."

"Do I look precious?"

"You really want me to answer that?"

Shira decides not to pursue that line of questioning any further, asking Leon, "So what do you want me to do?

"You'll be the point person on our operation" Leon says. "We've hired a local prostitute to do the luring but you'll be her partner in crime. We don't trust her to do it all alone. And having one of us seated at the table with her wouldn't be the look we're after either."

"And what look is that?"

"Two inebriated hot girls out on the town," Leon answers. "We want both of you seated near the bar in the Le Meridian Hotel, seemingly having a grand old time. When the target passes you on the way to get a nightcap, our prostitute will work her magic."

"Which is?"

"As if you didn't know," Leon responds with a wink. "But, enough chit-chat for now. We've rented a room on the same floor as Mr. El-Mashad's and here's the key."

"Our hired gun, so to speak, is already there," he continues, "presumably getting dressed, and probably steeling herself with alcohol as well. You'll find the outfit we picked out for you in the closet."

"Something elegant, I assume," Shira quips.

"Not even close," Leon answers.

"I say again, what do you actually want me to do?" Shira asks.

Leon looks at her incredulously. Does she really need him to tell her? But she looks so innocent, and beautiful, that he decides to humor her.

He answers, "Your first job is to make sure the prostitute isn't too blotto to do her job. And the second is to make her as attractive as possible, something we don't worry about with you, by the way. And third, by 8 o'clock, you need to have her down at a table in the dining room that we've reserved for the both of you. That's it. She'll take it from there."

Shira doesn't say anything for a few seconds. She's still trying to process what she thought Leon said. Not about her assignment but about her looks.

What was that about?

Finally, she regains her composure and asks, "How can we be positive that this "lady" we've hired will do her job? Which is what, by the way?"

"We've offered her an extra five hundred dollars," he replies, "if she can get into the room with him, get him undressed and comfortable, then open the door for us as she leaves."

"Is that enough money?"

"Well, for somebody who sells her body for less than a hundred dollars, that's big money."

"The question for me," Shira counters, "is can somebody who sells her body for less than a hundred dollars really be trusted to do this job? I should do it."

"Talk to Ari. He made the decision."

Shira watches closely as Leon Cohen ambles away.

He's a tall, good looking, late twenty-something guy, with sandy, curly hair that tumbles over his forehead, giving him a slightly boyish look. He seems harmless enough but she knows by reputation that he's anything but.

His face is ruddy, his smile crooked, his nose prominent, and his eyes twinkling with a sense of humor that has already been on display several times in the short time she's known him.

She finds herself wondering, "Is this him, the guy?" Even though he looks nothing like what she imagined her Prince Charming would look like. She thought dark. He's light-complexioned. She thought handsome. He's cute. She thought quiet. He seems garrulous, even under circumstances that don't exactly call for that. Still, there's something about him.

But, back to work, she thinks, looking at the room key in her hand. Better get up there quickly, before their "main attraction" gets too sloshed to be effective.

Once in the room, Shira realizes that she needn't have worried. The prostitute is totally sober and already dressed in the outfit provided for her.

Her name is Lauren Bassett, and she has a pixyish face with dimples and arched eyebrows. Her bosom is ample and highly visible, in a dress cut a little too low on the top and a little too high on the bottom. Obviously, some imaginative, young male agent, hopefully not Leon, picked it out but, on Lauren, it works. She looks seductive and available.

Shira's dress is more modest but not by much. It's a full-length scarlet cocktail dress with side slits that give the curious a small glimpse at her well-toned legs. Her breasts are smaller than Lauren's but just as much on display. When complemented by a simple pearl necklace, that does little to hide her décolletage, the look is striking, and not quite as in your face as what Lauren is wearing.

Together, they will attract attention that's for sure.

Shira notices that they still have a few minutes before showtime so she sits down on the sofa and pats the seat beside her. Lauren dutifully comes over and sits down.

"Why do you do what you do?" Shira asks Lauren the question that has been eating at her ever since she came into the room.

"Why do you?" Lauren counters with a question herself, in heavily accented English.

"The adventure, the unpredictability," Shira answers in French. "The sense that I'm doing something important."

"Same," Lauren answers, this time in French.

Realizing that the prostitute really doesn't want to have this conversation, Shira rises, looks at her watch and says, "Well, we better be going."

And the two head down to play their part in what will turn out to be one of the most audacious and controversial operations Mossad will ever do.

147

Before the night is over, Yahia el-Mashad, an Egyptian nuclear scientist who heads the Iraqi nuclear program, will be found dead in his hotel room at the Le Meridian Hotel in Paris, his head bludgeoned with a blunt object.

Witnesses will say that he was last seen in the bar area with two young women having a cocktail. None of them could recall exactly what happened after that but it was presumed Mr. el-Mashad left in the company of one, or both, of the girls.

His death is a major setback to Iraq's dreams of having a nuclear bomb capable of reaching Israel, and killing hundreds of thousands of its citizens, if not millions.

Chapter 13
Tel Aviv

"Answer me, Ari. Did you have anything to do with killing Lauren Bassett?"

Shira is referring to the mysterious death of the Parisian prostitute who she was partnered with in Paris. As reported in the paper, the poor girl died in a suspicious car accident just two weeks after the Egyptian nuclear scientist's murder.

"I'm serious. Did we eliminate her? Because if we did, I'm quitting," Shira shouts loudly enough for Eliana to get up from her desk in the hallway and shut the door to his office.

Ari stares at Shira without blinking, his squinty, bloodshot eyes focused squarely on her clear, translucent blue ones for a few seconds, then, he says quietly, "Well, in that case we didn't."

And he turns away, dismissing her.

Shira storms out of the room, furious, because the clear implication is that the Mossad did, in fact, eliminate Lauren Bassett for little or no reason. Just tidying up a few loose ends, as Ari likes to say.

"Are you OK?" Eliana asks, as her friend marches by.

"Not really," Shira tosses back over her shoulder.

When Shira gets back to her small desk in a cubicle located in the basement of Mossad headquarters, she calls personnel to get the number of Leon Cohen.

He'll be straight with her. She's sure of that.

She wants to find out about the prostitute's death, not because she was that close to her personally, but more because she shared an operation with Lauren and as any good spy knows, that creates an unusual bond.

The truth is that Shira is grieving, and she hopes Leon can ease the pain some.

When he calls her back, and she asks him the same question she'd asked Ari earlier, he answers cryptically, "I'm coming back to Tel Aviv tomorrow. Will you have dinner with me and I'll give you the whole story?"

They go to a cozy, but elegant restaurant, one that Shira is surprised Leon can afford on his Mossad salary. The decorating is a bit heavy-handed with thick tapestries on the walls, and dark oil paintings, probably prints, in ornate frames, scattered around the room. The tablecloths are purple-colored damasks, and there are unlit candles and fresh flowers on each table.

The look isn't awful. Just a little dated. An amalgam of old-world charm, with a few nouveau riche touches tossed in haphazardly in a futile attempt to modernize the place.

Still, to Shira, it reminds her of some of the upscale restaurants her parents took her to in Paris. And she's impressed that Leon chose it for their 'date.'

They're seated at a table upfront, maybe because the maitre'd thinks they'll class up the place. Or, more likely because he's saving the more discreet tables for his higher tipping patrons.

At Shira's request, Leon is talking about his life, something all agents are uncomfortable doing. She can't tell whether he's telling the truth or not. There's a chance he's drawing on his considerable operational experience playing other people to fabricate his story. But Shira doubts it.

What he's saying is just ordinary enough to be the truth. Humble beginning. Grew up in a kibbutz in the southern part of Israel. Paid his way through Tel Aviv University with an eye on joining the military after his schooling was finished. Majored in engineering and then, was planning to join the Combat Engineering Corps after graduation.

But, like Shira, Ari contacted Leon in his senior year and convinced him to give the Mossad a shot. He was reluctant at first but Ari was convincing, making the point that one operation by the Mossad could yield more real benefits for Israel than a dozen bridges built by engineers.

Then, in response to Leon's probing questions, Shira recounts her more exotic background, from Paris to Hebrew University in Jerusalem, medical training, and then, the Ari recruitment.

Both laugh at how alike their first impression of Ari was; a disheveled little man in a suit too big for him, trying to look inconspicuous on a campus full of rambunctious, young, and mostly underdressed, students.

They marvel that he could attract anybody to his cause, although, obviously, they were not immune to his understated charms themselves.

"Well, he was Mossad, after all," Leon says. "The guy looked like a nebbish until he told me who he was. Then, he became more intriguing. There must be something there, I thought."

"Ari? Intriguing?" Shira questions. "You still feel that way?"

"Well, I thought he could hardly be what he looked like and still work for the Mossad," he goes on. "And, yes, I still feel that way."

"Honestly, as a female, I thought he might be a dirty old man at first," Shira says, "out trolling for somebody he could bed."

Leon looks at her, a look of distaste on his face.

"He might still be," he says. "You ever think of that?"

"Plotz. I can't even imagine."

"I agree. He's a mensch if there ever was one," Leon says, giving Ari the compliment both know he deserves.

"A solid guy," he continues.

"So," Leon decides to change the subject, "thank you for your help in Paris."

"I didn't do much," she replies.

"Frankly, I was surprised that you didn't go to the hotel room with the prostitute. I thought you might want to push the envelope a little."

"You told me not to," Shira explains, "and the target didn't seem like a ménage a trois kind of guy."

"If he had been, would you have gone?" Leon says.

"My Mossad training taught me that you do whatever it takes. How about you?"

"How about me what?"

"Are you a ménage a trois kind of guy."

"Not me," Leon answers, "I'm a one woman guy all the way."

Then, Shira asks the obvious, but a-little-too-bold question.

"Do you have that one woman yet?"

"Nope. She hasn't come along," he answers.

"Well, for your sake, I hope she does soon," Shira says, while thinking to herself—*like right now.*

"So, about your question on the phone," Leon says, changing the subject from one that is uncomfortable for him, over to one that's even more uncomfortable.

"We had to. She threatened to blackmail us," Leon says bluntly.

"Lauren?"

"You were on a first name basis?" he asks.

"I spent a few minutes with her," Shira answers. "I liked her."

"That's too bad," Leon answers, "but nobody blackmails the Mossad."

It's true, Shira thinks. *If Lauren did that, Leon and his crew were left with no choice.* But, still, it doesn't make Shira feel any better about what happened. Or about her decision to join an agency as cruel as the Mossad.

****

The birds chirping outside her window awaken Shira. She feels amazingly rested and alive, given the shenanigans of the night before. She rolls over slowly, half-expecting to see the other side of her bed empty but there he is, still sleeping.

Leon's face is stubbled with the beginnings of a beard at least two shades darker than his hair. His eyes are closed, his lids puffy, perhaps from the two bottles of wine that they polished off over the course of the evening.

He's snoring slightly, his breath giving off a morning-after odor which is unpleasantly familiar to her. Still, to Shira, he looks unkempt and hairy, and wonderful. She wakes him up by pulling the covers away from his naked body and giving him a demure peck on the cheek. He opens one eye to look at her face, and then, at her body, half-covered by the sheets.

His expression goes from slightly irritated to curious to lustful in a matter of a few seconds.

Both eyes wide open now, Leon makes an abrupt lunge toward her, casting the covers aside, and grabbing her ankle as she playfully tries to wriggle away. They tumble off the bed, covers and all, into a squirming ball of arms, legs, and other body parts, reaching out in every direction. They are both laughing hysterically at the lunacy of their actions and what they must look like at the moment, all tangled up on the floor.

But then, the frivolity stops and the kissing, and caressing, begins. Their hands, legs, and lips are all incredibly active as they rush to find a mutual position that will accommodate them both, and facilitate the climax they both crave.

And, somehow, just in time, they make it happen.

Once sated, the giggles begin anew. Here are two reasonably mature adults, with responsible and dangerous jobs, acting like teenagers who are discovering the wonders of sex for the first time. And they can't stop laughing no matter what they do.

Finally, after passing their hands in front of their faces in an attempt to become serious again, then, laughing even more uproariously, Shira and Leon go into separate rooms just to stop the grinning.

That seems to work for a minute. But, when they come back, reasonably sober-faced, all they have to do is look at each other, before bursting into laughter again.

Later, when both are done with the fun and frivolity, and fully dressed, Leon re-introduces the subject of the operation they just completed.

"I don't know what Ari told you," he says, "but what we did in Paris was a really big deal. One of the most important Mossad operations ever."

"I know that."

"I honestly don't think the Iraqis will be able to complete their nuclear plan without el-Mashad," he goes on. "What we did was way more effective than sending planes to bomb their labs. From what I know, the one guy we killed was irreplaceable. And we didn't have to sacrifice a lot of innocent civilians to accomplish it. It was pretty surgical."

"Are you trying to justify what we did? Because, if you are, save your breath," Shira says. "I'm sure that, if Ari approved it, the operation was a necessary evil. And, at this point, I'm not one to second-guess his decisions."

"He approved the killing of the prostitute, too."

Shira arches her eyebrows and gives Leon a stern look.

"I thought we put that one to bed, also," she says.

"I wasn't so sure," Leon answers. "I don't want you to think that I enjoy that aspect of the job any more than you do. Because I don't."

"I already know that."

155

"Is there anything else you want to know about our operation?" he asks. "Because, after today, I'd rather not speak about it again."

"That's fine with me," Shira replies. "On to more pleasant things."

And she leans over to kiss him.

****

Everything is going swimmingly for Shira and Leon, romance-wise, until Aaron calls. He's apologetic about his behavior the last time they were together and wants to meet up again.

"I don't even know why I got so upset," he says. "I don't care what you do for a living. I just want to go back to the way we were."

"That might not be possible."

"I don't mean like back when we were kids," Aaron continues. "We both know too much now to ever be that carefree again. I mean where we can discuss things, even political things, without getting all upset."

"I'm seeing somebody," Shira says without emotion.

"OK. I guess that's not surprising," Aaron counters. "But maybe we can get together anyway, over drinks, like the old college friends we are. Reminisce a little. You can even tell me about him."

"That won't work, Aaron," Shira interrupts. "You know that. We're old lovers, not old friends."

"Can't old lovers become old friends?"

"Perhaps in time," she replies. "Let's just see how things play out. I'll give you a call when the time is right."

"OK. I'll be waiting."

Shira is surprised at the mixed emotions she feels as she hangs up the receiver. She was sure that any feelings she had for Aaron had been washed away in the torrent of emotions she felt for Leon. But she now knows that there's still something there. So, she better be careful.

Another complicating factor is that, after a brief flurry of activities that kept her fully engaged, Shira is bored again. Her love life may be exciting but the rest of her life is decidedly not, even with a man in it.

One thing about undercover agents is that they have a lot of free time between operations. And one of Ari's most difficult tasks is to find ways to keep his assets busy, and happy, when they're not out somewhere on assignment.

With Leon Cohen it's particularly hard. He's a man of action. Solid, engineering-type mind, well-organized, but quickly bored. Still, he has a wealth of hands-on experience that makes him valuable as a kind of consultant.

So, Ari has him meet with different teams before they go on operations, reviewing their game plans, testing their thinking. On occasion he even does post-ops reviews, and because he's so well-respected, the team members listen closely to his critiques.

Ari knows from experience that the reverse would not be true. Leon has a thinner skin than most casual acquaintances would think, and he can dish it out a lot better than he can take it. In fact, he's quick to anger, especially when he thinks he's dealing with people not as smart as he is. Which is often the case.

Shira, on the other hand, although just as stubborn as Leon in some ways, is a little more receptive to discipline overall, and a little more flexible, as well.

Perhaps it's her relatively young age or her respect for the chain of command but, whatever it is, Ari can give her mundane tasks that he wouldn't give other experienced agents, knowing full well that she'll do a good job, no matter how bored.

Right now, for instance, Ari has her on a desk reviewing and summarizing field reports. It's a little like Leonardo de Vinci touching up the work of first-year art students but the old spymaster really has no choice at this point, because, right now there are no available operations around that fit her unique skill set.

Shira and Leon have settled into a comfortable daily routine and although they haven't moved in together yet, they might as well have.

Some nights she stays at his place. Others he stays at hers. And some nights, particularly those Leon might have to work late with some ops team, they go home alone to their own apartments.

But, even on those nights, they spend a fair amount of time on the phone, not really talking so much as just staying connected, their conversations often book-ended by minutes of silence.

The relationship is unlike any Shira has experienced before, mainly because Leon is unlike any man she's ever known before. He's different than Howard, the med student she had a brief fling with. Not as much fun, perhaps, although amusing in his own way. And he's way different than Aaron, her most steady beau through the years. Just as intelligent, perhaps, but not very cerebral or introspective. Aaron is always thinking about something or other, but Leon only thinks when he's forced to by circumstances.

He does have a unique kind of "reactive street smarts," however, that makes him valuable as a partner on an operation but not as interesting romantically. Except for the sex.

Aaron found his way into Shira's panties by using his mind as an aphrodisiac. Leon isn't that subtle. When he wants something, he just goes after it and there are times when that suits Shira's mood just fine. But there are times when she would prefer a little verbal foreplay.

Shira hates to admit it but, with Leon, she misses Aaron's intellectual stimulation. Because Leon can be a little bit Neanderthal at times.

Finally, after months of mostly mundane assignments, Leon tells Shira that he has an assignment that will take him to Iraq for a few days. When she starts to ask questions, he holds his hand up.

"You know the drill. I shouldn't have told you where," he says.

"But you did. Are you part of Ammunition Hill?" she asks.

"What do you know about that?" he replies, obviously surprised at her knowledge about something so top secret.

"I am a spy after all," she says. "What we do is find out information nobody wants us to know. Remember?"

"Well then, Mata Hari, you better go back to your source and have a chat," Leon says, a grin on his face. "Because the operation isn't called Ammunition Hill

159

anymore, and you won't get any more out of me, no matter what."

"Are you sure?" Shira responds coquettishly, as she unbuttons the two top buttons on her blouse.

"My lips are sealed," he answers.

Another button. And, then, she bends over slightly, exposing just the pillowy curves of the tops of her beasts peeking over a light pink brassiere.

"OK, what do you want to know?" he cries. "I'll tell you everything."

But he doesn't, and Shira still gives him what he wants, mostly because it's what she wants also, and because, for the moment at least, why he's going to Iraq doesn't interest her any more.

The next morning, however, as she helps Leon pack, her curiosity emerges again. And she goes right back at him with the questions.

"Where are you flying into? Who's on the team? What's the objective? You want me to go with you?"

Leon just smiles. And, after a time, he says, "I should have followed my number one rule. Never mess around with somebody from the agency."

"Is that what we're doing? Messing around?"

"Bad choice of words, maybe. But you know as well as I do, that I can't divulge anything at this point. It's a job. That's all. We'll talk about it when I get back."

Shira makes an exaggerated pout. Then, she gives Leon a kiss that she hopes will keep her on his mind, no matter what he runs into in Iraq.

Later, after he's been gone for a few hours, she thinks about what Eliana told her about the situation in Iraq. The killing of el-Mashad slowed down their nuclear plans some but now they're back at it, or so she hears, and the word is that the government is again building a reactor that Mossad believes will eventually be used offensively against Israel.

Further, it's rumored that some of the engineers working on the project are non-Muslims who aren't as committed to Israel's destruction as the Iraqis are. Even better, they can be little loose-lipped at times. So, it doesn't take a nuclear scientist to guess that Leon is in Iraq to gather intel from one or more of them.

And Shira would like to be there with him.

Not only would it be another feather in her cap, career-wise but it would be an opportunity to work alongside her lover again, which is something she'd like to do more than ever.

She's been spending a lot of time with Leon, yes, but she knows from experience that the Leon in the field is an entirely different one than the unshaven guy who's been lying around her apartment the last few weeks, perusing newspapers, snacking, drinking beer, and lamenting how useless he's become.

That Leon has become tedious, and for the good of the relationship, she'd like to spend some more time with the other one.

Chapter 14
Baghdad

Leon Cohen slips into Baghdad disguised as a German banker attending a conference there. His German is passable, one reason he's been chosen for the assignment, but, as it turns out, he doesn't really have to speak it.

Leon's passport and papers are good enough that nobody at the airport questions him until he attempts to claim his luggage. Then, right at the baggage carousel, an armed policeman comes up to him and tries to interrogate him in Arabic. After listening to the guttural sounds being uttered in response, the guard tries English, a language he speaks well enough to get his point across.

He says he wants to review Leon's papers again.

Leon pulls them out of his carry-on and the guard makes a big deal out of inspecting each page in detail. Leon is convinced that something is wrong and has visions of being carted off to the infamously awful Baghdadi prison. Eventually, however, the guard reluctantly passes the papers back and lets Leon gather his luggage.

Still suspicious, however, he follows Leon through the outside double doors, out to the curb, where he stands around just long enough to make Leon incredibly uncomfortable.

Then, just as the guy approaches Leon again, Mossad agent Seymour Glazer pulls up to the curb and, reaching across the seat, throws the passenger door open.

Leon throws his bag into the back seat, slides quickly into the passenger seat, and the two leave the airport without looking back at the guard.

"What was that about?" Seymour asks.

"Maybe he doesn't trust Germans," Leon quips jocularly, hiding his fear.

"I wonder how he feels about Jews?"

"I'd rather not find out."

When they finally reach the hotel, Leon breathes a little easier but both agents are still a bit shaken by the encounter. So, after finding their room on the second floor, Seymour does a perfunctory search for listening devices. When he doesn't find any, the two spies breathe easier, thinking they are relatively safe. For the moment, at least.

Still, just to be sure, they go into the bathroom, turn on the tap water, and talk only loud enough to be heard by the other over the sound of flowing water.

"I'm not sure how much you know about the situation here, Leon," Seymour begins. "My asset is a lower-level engineer at the Osirak reactor, which is located in a southeast suburb of Baghdad."

"I know that."

"He's a Frenchman originally recruited by Yves Girard, the guy who designed the plant. But he got disillusioned when he learned more about some things they were constructing. So, he found his way to me."

"What things?"

"Well, for one," Seymour continues. "Although the reactor is ostensibly being built for energy purposes, my mole believes that a lot of money is being spent now that will facilitate the production of bombs later. His superiors tell everybody differently, but my guy's naturally suspicious."

"Damn," Leon answers. "And we know where those bombs will be headed. Right? Can we get photos or plans or anything else to back up his claim?"

"That's why you're here. My asset won't talk to us any further without assurances that he'll be adequately protected when the shit hits the fan."

"Did you give him those assurances?"

"Yes," Seymour answers, "but he wants them to come from somebody higher up, like you."

"But I'm not higher up."

"He doesn't know that, does he?" Seymour responds, "and, in your illustrious career, you've pretended to be just about every kind of guy I can imagine, good and bad. Surely, you can pretend to be Ari Lavon just for one meeting. Nobody knows the guy better than you do. Just act a little befuddled and absent minded."

"I'm much too tall and handsome to be Ari," Leon responds. "So, it'll be a stretch for me. But I can easily do the 'befuddled' part. You'll see."

The next day the two spies meet with Pierre Lafonte, the engineer Seymour has been courting, and tell him that, not only is Leon Cohen a very high up official in the Mossad, but that he has full authorization to arrange some kind of protection should Pierre's intel be actionable. They can warn him of any action ahead of time, yes, but even better they will whisk him away to some safe house if that becomes necessary."

The engineer is skeptical at first, not entirely convinced that Leon is who he says he is. But, Eventually, he's confident enough to continue the conversation.

"So, what do you want from me?" the Frenchman asks.

"Well, let's start with what makes you think the Iraqis are going to make nuclear bombs at your plant?"

"Just to be perfectly clear. I don't know for a fact that they're going to make bombs. I just think that, given some things they're doing now, they could at some later point."

"Like what things?"

"Well," Pierre answers. "There are a couple of rooms being built that, as far as I can tell, have no energy producing use. They look more like production facilities, in a word, factories, designed to build things. What, I don't know."

"Could be bombs, right?"

"You said that, not me. But the rooms are being built with the kind of safety features usually associated with handling fissionable materials."

"Can I see those rooms?" Leon asks.

"Hardly," the engineer answers. "Plant security is really tight at the moment and even if you have legitimate papers, the guards would be suspicious of anybody they don't already know. It's a pretty buttoned-up place. Nobody can just slip in without being noticed."

"Bullshit. It's a construction zone, for Christ's sake. There are contractors and laborers going in and out all the time. It can't be as buttoned-up as you say," Leon responds.

"I can get you blueprints and/or construction documents," Pierre says, "but I can't get you into the plant. Sorry. End of discussion. Finis."

"Actually, you're going to do both," Leon answers, feigning impatience, "or I can't do anything for you. Blueprints and construction documents aren't enough. I have to see the situation first-hand."

"Fine. Let's call the whole thing off. I don't need this shit anyway."

And, in the haughty manner shared by most Frenchmen since the beginning of time, he puts his nose and chin into the air, making him appear slightly taller than he is, sticks his chin out, and looks at the two men defiantly.

Then, he spins on his heels, and dramatically struts out of the room, slamming the door behind him. Or tries to, but the pneumatic door stop cushions the impact, making the exit even more comical.

Leon starts laughing but not Seymour.

"I've been romancing this guy for months," he says after Pierre leaves. "And in a few short minutes, you've managed to alienate him to the point where we'll never get anything out of him."

"Yes, we will," Leon replies. "I'm betting he figures out a way to get me into the plant. But, if not, you'll just apologize to him. Tell him I'm a jerk, and that the documents he's provided will work fine."

"You don't know Pierre."

"I know his type."

And, fortunately, Leon turns out to be right. The next morning Pierre calls Seymour back to tell him that, although it's risky, he's figured out a way to smuggle Leon in if they really want to attempt it.

The Frenchman says he's filched the badge of a member of the clean-up crew which Leon can use until six that evening so it can be returned to the rightful owner in time for the night shift.

Armed with the badge, Leon is able to get onto the site easily, and to see for himself what made Pierre question the plant's real purpose in the first place.

Despite a largely superficial effort to hide what the plant is all about, to Leon's less-educated but astute eye, Pierre is absolutely right.

The Iraqis intend to build bombs here.

That night the two agents celebrate the success of their mini-operation by downing a few drinks in the hotel bar.

"Well done, Leon," Seymour says in a short, impromptu toast, and then, they click glasses. "You've still got it."

"Couldn't have done it without you, partner."

"Are you heading back to Tel Aviv tomorrow morning?"

"No, couldn't get a reservation," Leon replies. "I'm on an evening flight. So, I have a day of R&R."

"Good," Seymour says. "In that case, I've got a special treat for you. The Iraqi President, Saddam Hussein, will be appearing in a parade tomorrow and we should be there."

"Why?"

"Well, for one thing, there've been seven assassination attempts on his life already and this parade is the perfect opportunity for the eighth. Wouldn't you like to see that?"

"You're not saying that we're—"

"No. No. Not by us," Seymour says. "It's just that he has more enemies inside Iraq than outside it. And this kind of event attracts enemies."

"Like us," Leon says with a grin and they click glasses again.

So, the next morning, the two spies take a kind of busman's holiday and find a way to blend into the Baghdad crowd. They're still undercover, of course, but now they're impersonating spectators who are just there to watch the show.

And what a show it turns out to be.

Saddam arrives in a suit, with a dark shirt, drab tie, and fedora, looking like a normal businessman might, except that he's carrying a long rifle, which he fires into the air as a signal for the parade to begin.

Then, with the band playing the new National Anthem of Iraq, and hundreds of soldiers marching toward their leader in lock-step, their arms swinging above their shoulders in a move reminiscent of Nazi parades, the parade begins.

Several divisions of men, some clad in dress blues or camouflage, and others in all white uniforms, many with their faces covered by a kerchief, pass the review stand in formation, holding their weapons straight up toward the sky or horizontally across their bodies. Fighter planes fly low over the square, followed by large transport planes, and then, attack helicopters. The ground shakes, and the noise is deafening and scary.

"This is awesome," Leon says to Seymour. "I'm glad I could stick around for it."

Every so often, Saddam Hussein fires his rifle into the air again, its sound muffled by everything else going on in front of him. To Leon, although it is certainly impressive pageantry, the whole thing is a bit comical as well.

This unbelievable display of military, with everything heavy and huge and loud, being commanded by what looks like an accountant, sporting a droopy, dense, black mustache, and carrying a comparatively tiny little pop gun that he fires randomly into the air above the crowd.

The highlight of the event, however, is the impressive weaponry. Huge, sleek, highly polished missiles roll past, followed by tanks and mobile cannons. Interspersed between the armored military vehicles, are legions of different kinds of soldiers, all bedecked in colorful uniforms.

The vaunted Royal Guard bring up the rear, dressed unlike any of the soldiers who came before them. With pointed gold helmets and flashy uniforms sporting bold splashes of both red and gold epaulets. They are the last line of defense should anybody ever try to overthrow Saddam. And, in dress and demeanor, they look perfectly capable of doing the job.

"I'm impressed," Leon whispers, "you would think this was Russia or China or the United States. Not a small Arab country with limited resources."

"Now do you see why it's critical that we keep Saddam Hussein from getting nuclear weapons," Seymour says. "This guy is an egomaniac, a despot who craves power more than most I've seen around the Middle East. Which, is saying something. Oh, and he hates Jews."

"Who in this region doesn't"

"Even worse," Seymour goes on. "I think he has a screw loose and if given the opportunity, he wouldn't hesitate to spray nuclear bombs around like he's spraying bullets today, from that little rifle of his."

"Now, I understand why there have been so many attempts on his life," Leon says. "And, honestly, if I had a gun on me right now, I'd take my chances from here."

"If you had a gun on you, partner, you'd already be dead," Seymour responds.

Chapter 15
Tel Aviv

That evening, Leon boards a commercial flight, confident that the documents and first-hand observations he's bringing with him will be enough to trigger some kind of Israeli action against the plant.

But first, after arriving at the Tel Aviv airport, he has to survive the barrage of questions thrown his way by Shira, who greets him as he deplanes.

She starts innocently enough, "How was Baghdad?"

"Very nice. Good shops, restaurants. A wonderful respite."

"Did you do anything but eat, drink, and be merry."

"Nope."

"Did you see Saddam's palace?" She asks. "I hear it's quite something."

"Wouldn't know. He didn't invite us over."

"Who were you with?"

Obviously, Shira isn't going to let it just go. She's determined to find out what he did and why.

"Seymour Glazer," he replies. "A friend from work. You know him?"

"Is he stationed there?" she asks, ignoring Leon's question.

"Look, Shira," Leon says. "If we're going to make this dalliance of ours work, you have to respect my space and I'll respect yours. There are things you can't tell me, like what you did in Beirut, and things I can't tell you, like what I did in Baghdad."

"First, you say we're messing around. Now we're having a dalliance. Is that all this is to you?" Shira asks.

"I don't know why I said that. I don't even know what it means," Leon says. "But the truth is that we have fun together, enjoy each other's company. And the sex is terrific. Do we need any more than that?"

Shira just stands there looking at Leon, saying nothing, for a few long minutes. Then, a large tear starts to trickle down her cheek. Then another. Then a lot of tears. And her mascara begins to run.

Finally, she blurts out, "I guess I do," and turns away from Leon, first walking and then running toward the exit and parking garage.

"I think I'll taxi home," Leon says to no one in particular.

The next day Leon spends the whole day in briefings. First Ari. Then, Yitzhak Hofi. Followed by high-level military leaders and selected members of the Knesset.

Meanwhile Shira sits at her desk in another part of Mossad headquarters rethinking her life.

I now understand why Aaron got so upset when I wouldn't tell him anything, she thinks. *Still, he's a civilian, not cleared for the kind of intel I deal with. I can't share my*

172

work with him. But Leon? We're in the same line of work
for God's sake. He should trust me.

"Shira, are you done with that report yet."

The voice seems to come from another planet. But, it's
her interim boss, the woman across the room who runs the
administrative department of Mossad.

"Should have it in a few minutes," Shira replies,
realizing that she's done nothing for over a half-hour now,
other than fret, brood, and feel sorry for herself. So, putting
her feelings on the back burner, she focuses on the mundane
task at hand.

Leon Cohen, on the other hand, has given no thought to
his relationship with Shira at all. He's been too busy
answering questions.

"Why would you think they could turn those rooms into
a bomb production line?" an overly-smug minister of
something or other asks. "Have you even seen a factory that
makes bombs?"

"No," Leon answers, "but what other purpose could
those rooms serve? They're far too large for conference
rooms. And the ceilings are three times as high as a normal
room. And they're installing skylights, vents, and industrial
sized exhaust fans."

"I just wish somebody with better credentials had taken
a look at them," the minister counters.

"Somebody did, remember?" Leon responds. "Our
asset, the French engineer. He's the one who suspected a
manufacturing facility in the first place."

"How trustworthy is he?"

"Well," Leon answers, "That's why you sent me. To confirm his credibility. And I think he's legit."

The government official still isn't convinced.

"Most importantly" Leon continues. "I brought proof. You don't have to believe me. Just show my pictures to somebody you trust. An independent expert. Get a third opinion, if you want."

"We will. Believe me, we will."

Leon knows that the decision he's asking the higher ups to make is a difficult one. In fact, his input and arguments are just the beginning of the debate. Many of those who will make the decision don't think the evidence is enough to warrant a military strike. But others do.

And Leon expects that the discussion will go on for months.

For today, however, the talking does end, but eventually Prime Minister Begin decides that, under the new code name Operation Opera, eight Israeli F-16 fighter planes and six Israeli 15-A's will attack the Osirak nuclear plant in a daring three-hour mission, effectively destroying any capability for Iraq to create nuclear bombs in that facility.

No matter how inconclusive it seemed at the time, Leon's intel is the deciding factor in this highly controversial operation, which, although effective, is heavily criticized by the U.N., and dozens of other international players, even including Ronald Reagan, the President of the United States.

The rocky relationship between Leon and Shira has been an on-again off-again affair for months now, partially because they're seldom in the same place at the same time. Also, because they've settled into a "don't ask, don't tell" policy regarding anything professional, and that has limited the couple's ability to have long, meaningful conversations of any kind. As a result, there's a lack of trust building up, and nothing else is as toxic to a relationship.

They seem to be compatible only when they're in bed.

In fact, ironically, as their love is dying out, their passion has grown proportionally, as if to fill the gap.

Like sailors on shore leave, when Shira and Leon come home to Tel Aviv, they tend to smoke too much, drink too much, and make love way too much.

Eventually, though, even the sex can't keep them together, and they drift apart without ever truly acknowledging what caused it, if they even knew.

****

When Shira arrives at the small waiting area outside Ari's office, she's surprised to find Leon already there waiting.

"What are you doing here?" she asks.

"I could ask you the same thing."

There's a long, uncomfortable silence.

The two estranged lovers haven't spoken to each other in months. Neither has felt the need to try to patch things up. They seem to be comfortable just acting like agents who once worked with each other.

So, Shira sits down in the only other chair, which is uncomfortably close to Leon's and looks away, as if she's interested in the boring print on the far wall. Anything to keep from having a conversation with him.

Eliana offers them both coffee but her offer falls on deaf ears. She can sense the tension, and understands the reasons for it.

"Well, just let me know," she says to no one in particular.

"Do you think he knows about us?" Shira whispers to Leon without looking at him.

"I haven't told anybody. Have you?"

Just then, Ari comes out of the office and greets his two agents warmly. Grabbing each by the elbow, he escorts them into his office and motions them to sit down in the two chairs pulled up in front of his desk.

Then, he shuts the door and locks it.

The old spymaster can't shed old habits. Even here in the bowels of Mossad headquarters, with security as tight as anywhere in Israel, Ari likes to talk about his operations quietly, behind locked doors, with his audience huddled closely around his desk.

But Shira moves her chair a little further away from Leon anyway.

"Well, well," he begins. "Are we keeping you two busy?"

"Hardly," Leon answers, although given recent operations that fit his skills more than hers, he's certainly been busier than Shira.

"That's about to change," Ari says cryptically. "Have you ever been to Sudan?"

"Not recently," Leon answers. "Why? Is there anything there?"

"Just some Ethiopian Jews," Ari answers, "trying to escape a civil war and the genocide that has followed."

"Ethiopian Jews?" Shira asks, with a quizzical expression on her face.

"Yes," Ari replied. "For centuries there have been Jewish communities known as Beta Israel, living peacefully in hundreds of villages in Northern Ethiopia. But, with the unrest there, they've been leaving in droves, crossing hundreds of miles of desert on foot, trying to find sanctuary in Sudan or somewhere else."

"What does that have to do with us?" Leon asks.

"We've decided to launch a top-secret operation, code-named Operation Brothers, to help those refugees come to Israel," Ari continued, "And I want you two to be a part of it."

"Not a normal Mossad operation, is it?" Leon asks haughtily. "And not exactly my speed either. I'd rather be undercover in Syria or Egypt or somewhere a little more important, if you don't mind. Where I can make a difference."

"Sudan is just as Muslim as Syria or Egypt," Ari counters. "And they may even hate us more."

"Still," Leon argues. "It's not exactly a frontline battleground for us now, is it?"

"Listen, Leon," the spymaster replies. "This operation is riskier than, say, using a prostitute to lure an Egyptian scientist to a Parisian hotel room. And, honestly, it could prove to be way more important than that as well."

"Why us?" Shira decides to divert the discussion.

"I just think this operation would be less suspicious if a husband and wife were involved," Ari answers. "You two can fake it, can't you?"

He smiles knowingly and the two ex-lovers exchange a quizzical glance.

"Oh, come on. Did you really think a guy who's been in the spy business as long as I have would miss the obvious signs?"

"We're not together anymore," Shira protests.

"I know that, too, but you've got some experience to draw on. Am I right?"

Getting no answer, Ari launches into his always succinct description of what he would like them to do. Leon and Shira will be one of two "European" couples who will establish a scuba diving resort in eastern Sudan, under the auspices of a Swiss travel company. At least that's what the Sudanese government will be told.

In actuality, the resort will be the pickup point for an Israeli navy operation that will transport hundreds of Ethiopian refugees up the Red Sea to Israel.

"Sounds simple," Leon says. "Except for the part about us doing this without Sudan knowing."

"They will know—" Ari answers, "—about the diving resort. In fact, the couple heading up this venture are in Khartoum right now negotiating a three-year lease agreement with Sudan's Tourism Ministry, which will include government support, and protection. The Sudanese just won't know about the smuggling part."

"So, once they agree," Shira asks, "all we have to do is build a resort, pretend it's real, then move refugees through it, as if they're tourists, and keep the Sudan government from knowing what we're actually doing?"

"No," Ari answers. "Here's the beauty of the plan. The resort already exists. It was established as "Arous on the

178

Red Sea" by an Italian company over a decade ago but it's been dormant for years now. You're just going to activate it."

"As an Israeli navy base?" Leon asks.

"No. As a fully operative scuba diving resort, with tourists and everything. It's just that on occasion, at night, as a little sidelight, you'll help hundreds of refugees escape the tyranny of Ethiopia, and possible imprisonment by the Sudanese."

"Piece of cake," Shira mutters under her breath.

"What was that?" Ari inquires.

"She's expressing her enthusiasm for the idea," Leon interjects.

Chapter 16
Sudan

"Who thought up this crazy idea?" Leon asks just seconds after meeting Yola Reitman and Gad Shimron, their new partners in crime.

"I did," Gad answers, with a big smile on his face. "Pure genius, huh?"

Leon and Shira have just arrived at Khartoum International Airport and are being met at the gate by the couple who they'll be working with over the next few months.

The two Mossad agents are hardly what Shira expected. Both are fair-skinned with light curly hair and surprisingly young faces, not that Shira can complain about that. It's just that she expected somebody to be the adult in the room, knowing full well that she and Leon wouldn't be.

Adding to her concern is that both are smiling crazily, as if to say, is this a great adventure or what? Looking around the third-world airport and thinking about the task ahead, Leon and Shira are not so convinced that it will be all fun and games. It may, in fact, be more dangerous than any other operation they've done.

"So, I'm curious—" Shira starts.

"Save it for when we're in the car," Gad interrupts, looking around with a conspiratorial look on his face which is probably exaggerated, purely for their entertainment.

The drive from Khartoum to the Red Sea is long, dusty, and boring, especially in the old, dirty, drafty Jeep that Gad and Yola apparently rented, or commandeered from some sympathetic Sudanese worker.

They follow the Nile River for a while, then cut through uninhabited sandy stretches of nothingness, before finally reaching a small mountain range that seems to protect the Red Sea. Nothing but uninterrupted sand, sun, and glare greet them along the way. So, with not much scenery to look at, and little in common, the two couples decide to spend the time in the car getting acquainted.

Shira discovers that both she and Gad are graduates of the Hebrew University in Jerusalem, and that he has worked on and off for the Mossad for several years now. He's an avid scuba diver, which obviously played a role in his choosing to create a resort catering specifically to divers.

Yola has been a stewardess for El Al Airlines for the last few years, but has also helped the Mossad out occasionally, when her ability to move freely between European cities and her language skills, proves advantageous.

She took a leave of absence from the airlines, she says, when Gad, her diving instructor, recruited her to join him in what he sees as "one of the greatest humanitarian opportunities ever," and one uniquely appropriate to their skills.

"He can be quite convincing," she says.

"He'll have to be," Leon responds, probably referring to his own doubt about the whole idea of running a very commercial resort, while engaging in clandestine rescue operations at night.

"I admit that there are some details to be worked out," Gad says, "but the refugees are already pouring into overcrowded, disease-infested, camps around our property. We just can't let them suffer, and die, while we try to make everything perfect."

How imperfect things actually are, becomes clear when Shira and Leon finally arrive and see the so-called "resort" for the first time.

It consists of a rather large, one-story, dilapidated, red-tile-roofed building with two lines of small, bungalows feeding out on either side from the main structure, a dozen or so feet apart, and all paralleling the coastline.

The place may have been "charming" at one time but it certainly isn't now. All the two new agents can see is the enormous amount of work the place needs before anybody would stay there.

"The camps can't be worse than this," Shira comments.

"Maybe we should try to just make the camps better," Leon suggests, "and forget about this place."

"Now, Leon, you're making us feel bad," Yola responds, feigning hurt feelings. "We've been working on this place for months now, and to us, it's very nice compared to what it was. Almost four-star."

"And we have electricity, too," Gad adds. "We finally got the generators up and running yesterday."

"So, I can take a hot bath?" Shira asks.

"Absolutely," Gad answers, "Sometime later this week."

And, with a smile, Yola clarifies, "When the water trucks arrive."

Leon looks at Shira's crestfallen expression and begins to laugh. Within seconds Shira is laughing with him and their two new best friends can't help but join in.

Before long all four of them are sitting, or lying, on the ground, alternately guffawing and crying, not just at the hopelessness of the situation all around them, but also at themselves for thinking they were in any way qualified to take on this task. The impromptu giggle session proves to be cathartic, bonding, and absolutely necessary for them to come together as a team.

When they finally do gain control of their emotions, it's with a shared sense of purpose, like they've stripped away all the pretense, and there's nothing but pent-up passion and energy left. Not to mention a touch of naïveté.

Nobody else is around to do the job, so without actually saying it, they all decide at that moment to metaphorically roll up their sleeves and get to work.

The next few weeks are a frenzy of activity, made a little easier by the capable Sudanese staff hired by Gad and Yola, which are eight enthusiastic, highly-driven employees who feel as much like owners as the four managers do.

And, over time, although never told the true purpose of the resort, they become highly motivated to make the thing work. They are truly part of the team.

There are six bedrooms in the main clubhouse but, to protect their cover identities, each of the two couples choose just one to share, leaving the four others for extra management personnel that they intend to hire along the way. It will be cozy but comfortable in a Bohemian kind of way.

The first few nights they cook their own meals over an open fire in the so-called parking lot. But, finally, after getting electricity, they're able to make the kitchen functional, and begin tryouts for a head chef and cooks.

The meals do improve after that, as they, and the various chef candidates, experiment with dishes that will be featured in the dining room once the resort is officially open.

Each night, after the staff has left and dinner is over, the two young couples are left alone in the clubhouse, with hardly any lighting and no entertainment, except what unlimited booze, and their own personalities, can provide.

So, naturally, it doesn't take them long to discover the joys of cavorting in the Red Sea at night, often in skimpy bathing suits, sometimes with nothing on at all, and with only the moonlight to guide their way around the reefs and through the surf. It proves to be cathartic.

Gad and Yola are not only wonderful swimmers but skilled scuba divers as well, and they are at home in the water.

Leon and Shira, on the other hand, although strong physically, aren't nearly as confident in their ability to swim. So, they spend more time close to the shore, just splashing about, and body surfing, with the beach always close at hand so they can get out of trouble if necessary.

What the two couples don't know yet, as they labor mightily in the day, and party heartily at night, is that once the resort is open, and Operation Brothers is fully underway, the fun is over. From that point on, it will be all work, with a little bit of tension added, just for seasoning.

Shira finds she is in her element. Not only are the spats with Leon a thing of the past but she loves the focus, simplicity, and purpose of her life right now. She's in a good place, and is happy to have Leon join her there.

Their hotel is called the Red Sea Diving Resort, and they have begun to advertise it all across Europe. Brochures have been printed and distributed. Travel agents have been alerted. And dozens of groups are actually booking this brand-new experience. Success is in sight.

At this point, the two couples have been joined by a few other Mossad agents, but the management structure is as it has been from the beginning.

Yola is the General Manager of the resort, manning the front desk, handling reservations, taking care of requests, supervising the kitchen, and essentially, acting like the face of the place. She is assisted by one of the new agents and a young Sudanese.

Gad is the Activities Manager, running the exercise classes in the morning, taking guests out on diving trips in the afternoon, and organizing occasional field trips or game nights. He now has two other instructors under him, both of which are eager to receive actual guests.

Leon is the Facilities Manager, and designated handyman during the day but, much more importantly, when the guests have retired for the night, he is in charge of the refugee pickups, and he coordinates the Navy rendezvous operations. All of the Mossad agents report to him at night, and operate in two shifts, one night on and one off.

Shira acts as Operations Manager, supervising the housekeeping crew, handling transportation, and making sure that, no matter their responsibilities, nobody interferes with the nightly assignments.

The team is organized, confident, and more than ready when the first bus of German tourists arrives. But it turns out their confidence is misplaced. What worked perfectly in practice doesn't work at all in actuality.

After the eight-hour bus ride, the Germans are tired, angry, and quite underwhelmed by their first look at the place. Their displeasure generates lots of angry looks, and complaints, spoken in a guttural language only Leon can understand.

Not surprisingly, the two guest bathrooms in the main clubhouse are popular first stops for everybody. So, lines form there immediately. As they do at the check-in desk where Yola is completely swamped. Everybody just wants to get their keys, go to their cottages, unpack their bags, and lay down on their beds to rest after their long trip from Khartoum.

Shira jumps in to serve as backup at the desk but, with only one credit card imprint machine, she isn't much help. They are captive to the machine. Before long, people lose their patience, and begin wandering around outside to take a look at the beach, the outdoor accommodations, and the main attraction, the beautiful Red Sea.

It's disorganized chaos. Not at all the way the four young managers imagined it. Obviously, they will have to space the arrivals better in the future so their staff can deal with the process in a more systematic way. But, right now, they are coping as best they can.

One man keeps shouting an expression that Leon interprets as meaning, "Where the hell is the bar?"

So, being the most resourceful of the lot, he stops carrying luggage in from the bus, grabs a Vodka bottle from the liquor closet, and starts pouring free shots to anybody in line. Soon after that, Gad follows his lead by handing out cans of cold beer as well, and snacks.

"I've never seen a problem that alcohol won't take the edge off," Leon says to Gad.

And it turns out he's right.

By the time everybody is checked in, unpacked, and back at the main clubhouse for dinner, the mood has improved considerably.

A few nights later, unbeknownst to the guests who are sleeping comfortably after a full day of exercise and scuba diving, the maiden voyage of the refugee evacuation takes place a little further down the beach, and it doesn't go according to plan either.

Earlier, Yola had bribed the Police Chief with a case of liquor to make sure his guards wouldn't bother the resort trucks as they traveled to and from the coast. It was a typical Sudanese business transaction. But there was a miscommunication and some of the actual guards didn't get the word.

So, on one of the early trips, with a dozen refugees on board, two guards wave the truck to stop at a closed gate. Fortunately, the two soldiers leave their weapons behind as they saunter over to inspect the truck when it stops. They are assuming it will just be a normal transaction in their country, a little bribery for a little favor.

But, halfway to the gate, they realize that the old truck has no intention of stopping. In fact, Leon accelerates through the gate, sending chunks of wood and metal flying everywhere. The refugees in the back, unprepared for the sudden change in speed, fall all over themselves, and end up in a tangled heap at the back of the truck. Panic sets in, and everybody is yelling, loud enough for the guards to hear.

"Quiet," Leon yells, "Shut up."

Fortunately, when the guards do realize what's happening, it's too late for them to scramble back for their guns, aim, and fire accurately at the truck as it roars past.

So, when they do get their guns, one of the guards misses entirely, his bullets kicking up dust behind the truck a few times. The other one's weapon misfires, and frustrated, he throws it aside as he shakes his fist at the intruders, as if that will help.

The next morning, while most of the hotel guests are out scuba diving, the two guards, and their supervisor, arrive unannounced to see if the old truck sitting out in front of the resort is, indeed, the same one that ran the checkpoint.

It is, of course but, because there are no bullet holes to prove it, the guards tell their boss it must be the wrong truck. They don't want him to think they missed it entirely from such close range.

Later that day, Gad delivers a few more bottles to the guards as a kind of "thank you" gift, and, from then on, the resort's trucks are allowed go to and from the beach on a fairly unimpeded basis.

But the operation transferring refugees to the Israeli Navy ships isn't going as smoothly. Sometimes there are too few boats to carry them and sometimes there are too many. Or none at all. And a water taxi operation that should take less than an hour often stretches well into the early morning hours.

And, even, on one occasion, a few Sudanese soldiers arrive near the end of the operation and start shooting at the departing boats.

Fortunately, Leon is able to intervene, and convince the patrol leader that a few of the resort's important guests wanted to scuba dive at night, when the most exotic fish and sea animals feed.

"Are you crazy," he yells. "A French politician is in one of those boats. You're going to create an international scandal that will end your career."

Eventually, the soldiers back off, never suspecting that just around the end of the cove, only a few hundred yards away, a darkened military ship lies at anchor, waiting to receive its nightly quota of refugees.

****

Everybody is busy, and tired. But happy.

Shira's relationship with Leon couldn't be better. They are, for all intents and purposes, a happily married couple, going their separate ways during the day, and sometimes even at night, but finding enough time together at times to make it all worthwhile.

They've "saved" hundreds of Jewish Ethiopians and everybody back at headquarters seems pleased.

If truth be told, many of those who endorsed the operation did so reluctantly, and few expected it to be this successful. Now, of course, everybody is saying it was their idea.

So, life is great—until Miriam Schwartz arrives.

"I'm here to replace you," she says to Shira, as she gets out of the car that brought her from the Khartoum Airport to the Red Sea Diving Resort.

"And who are you again?"

"I'm Miriam, a new agent. I've been in training with Ari for several months now," Miriam answers. "You should feel honored, by the way. He says he brought me on board because of your success. Not that I could ever measure up to the amazing things you've done."

"Who's this?" Yola shouts from the front door. "Some more help?"

"Not exactly," Miriam answers, even louder than Yola. "I'm from headquarters, here to replace Shira."

"She doesn't need a replacement," Yola responds as she approaches the new arrival. "Nor do we. Things are going very well, thank you. But, if you want to stay, we could use some help in the kitchen."

"Ari needs Shira back in Tel Aviv," Miriam explains. "He has another assignment for her. Something he says only she can do."

"Why didn't he tell us you were coming?"

"Maybe because he felt you might resist," Miriam says, the sarcasm apparent to all. "But I'll be glad to help out in the kitchen if that's what you want me to do."

Just then Leon comes around the corner, shirtless, with a tool belt thrown over his shoulder. Shira is very aware of how good he looks, hair bleached out, body tanned and toned from all the exercise and work.

Miriam is well aware, too.

"What have we here?" Leon asks, looking over the new arrival from head to toe.

"My replacement," Shira answers.

"You're kidding. Why are you being replaced? We need you here," he asks Shira.

"Beats me. This woman says Ari has another assignment for me."

"Really? What could be more important than this?" He asks. "Why break up the team at this point. We're just getting started, and I've never heard of a battlefield change taking place just when the battle is getting underway. It makes no sense."

Shira is pleased to hear Leon come to her defense.

"You'll have to talk to Ari," Miriam says. "For some reason, he needs Shira back in Tel Aviv. And I've got the official transfer papers here. And Shira's airline ticket as well."

With nothing more to learn from the agent who's replacing her, and with no way to argue with Ari, Shira realizes she has no choice. So, she goes back to the bedroom she shares with Leon and reluctantly starts to pack.

If I hurry, she thinks, *I can use the car Miriam arrived in without having to book one myself.*

A few minutes later Leon comes into the bedroom carrying Miriam's two pieces of luggage, and tosses them in the corner. Obviously, he expects her to move in with him.

"Really?" Shira says. "I'm still here."

"No other place for her to stay, love," Aaron. "But we'll reconnect when I get back to Tel Aviv. I shouldn't be here much longer."

Fat chance of that, Leon, Shira says under her breath, *I'm not falling for your macho charms again. Have fun with what's her name.*

Then she high-fives the team as she leaves, her eyes glistening with tears. Once in the car, however, her mind turns to whatever Ari wants her to do now. It must be important.

Chapter 17
Tel Aviv

Shira can't imagine why Ari would need her so immediately. There isn't a hostage situation that she knows of. And going back to Beirut isn't an alternative.

Oh well. I'll know soon enough, she tells herself.

The next day Shira's sitting at a Formica topped table in a small diner near Mossad headquarters, expecting Ari to join her any minute. She's peeved. No matter what assignment he has in mind, she won't just accept it, like some trained puppy dog.

Why didn't Ari talk to me before summoning me home? Don't I have a say in my assignments? After all I've done for him? And how can a totally inexperienced agent replace me anyway?

It slowly dawns on Shira that she isn't really as angry at Ari as she is at Leon. And his reaction. Or, more appropriately, his nonchalant non-reaction. She's jealous, and hurt.

How could he discard me so easily? She asks herself. *I was convinced that he was my guy, my soulmate. Then he's like, you're my new partner, Miriam? Fine. See you, Shira. Part of the job. Whatever, Leon, you jerk.*

Then, she's pulled back to reality.

"Shira, you look marvelous," Ari says as he slides into the booth across from her. "Living the dream in Sudan, huh? Nothing to do but sun, surf, and scuba dive."

"And save hundreds of refugees. Remember?"

"Oh yes, that too," Ari responds. "Wonderful job by you and the team, by the way."

"The job's not finished," Shira says pointedly.

"For you, it is," Ari counters. "I've got something more important for you to do and frankly, you're the only one who can do it."

"I'm all ears."

"You remember that guy you broke up with?"

"You mean the one you made me break up with?" Shira responds.

"OK. Semantics," Ari says. "We have it on good authority that he's been cooperating with the enemy."

"What enemy?" Shira asks.

"Egypt. Evidently, he was passing on information to them at a very inopportune time. At least we have a confidential informant who claims that."

"So, you don't know it for a fact?" Shira asks.

"Well, that's where you come in," Ari answers. "I need you to use your considerable charms to rekindle the relationship and see what you can find out for us."

At first, Shira is stunned.

Is there no limit to what the Mossad will ask me to do? Act like you're married to this guy. Act like you love this other guy. What makes me any different than the prostitute in Paris?

But, on second thought, now that her affair with Leon is over, she would be calling Aaron anyway. And why not find out for sure if he's a good guy or bad guy in the process? For her and the Mossad. She can kill two birds with one stone.

"OK. I'll do it," she says to Ari.

It turns out Shira doesn't have to call Aaron. He reaches out to her first, and she agrees to have dinner with him at one of their favorite haunts on the east side of Tel Aviv.

"Wow, do you look good. Been vacationing?" he asks right away.

"Hardly. I've been working at a resort," she answers, truthfully. "On the Red Sea."

"Doing what?"

"Kind of a manager. And kind of a housekeeper," she replies. "Not much pay but lots of perks."

"Looks like the perks include some outside activities."

"You got that right. Great beach. Incredible scuba diving. Even exotic field trips. A real unique experience. Glad I did it," Shira says. "How about you?"

"Same old same old," Aaron responds. "Trying to get stubborn people to look beyond their prejudices and do some business."

"Arabs?"

"Both sides, actually," Aaron says, adding, "Sometimes the best I can do is just get everybody to the table, with little chance for agreement. It gets pretty disheartening at times."

Shira decides it's too early in their newly rekindled relationship to probe any further. So, she changes the subject, and moves the conversation to safer ground.

"Ever hear from any of our old classmates?" she asks.

Her question leads to a long discussion about the behavior and quirks of people they knew in school. Like the guy who tested so high in the school entrance exam, they allowed him to set his own curriculum and work at his own pace.

"Flunked out his sophomore year, as I recall," Shira says.

"First semester," Aaron responds, and they both laugh.

Soon, just like the old days, the two of them are talking short hand, as if they had never been apart.

They remember their trips to the Muslim Quarter of Jerusalem and how scared they were to be in what seemed like a foreign country at the time. They remember how they would meet late at night, after study hours, to share a beer and a kiss before going to bed. And they talked about the few teachers they shared, and how differently they saw them at the time.

"Mr. Abelman. What an awful man," Shira said.

"Sweetheart of a guy," Aaron countered. "Gave me an "A" I didn't deserve."

"Tried to look up my skirt."

"So did I. And about every other guy in our class."

"Didn't really need to hear that," Shira said, feigning shock.

To her, it's surprising how easy flowing their conversation is, especially in contrast to the grunts, nods, and vacant stares she's been getting from Leon recently.

The evening ends abruptly, at the curb outside the cafe, where Aaron gives a Shira a tentative kiss, just like he did on their very first date.

Shira looks into his eyes, squeezes his hand, then, turns around and hails a cab, her heart aflutter in a way she hasn't experienced in years.

Maybe it took a fling with a fellow spy, she thinks, *to get my head screwed on straight. From now on, it's normal guys for me.*

Then, she remembers that Aaron may not be all that normal.

When Shira gets back to her apartment the phone is already ringing. And, not surprisingly, Ari is on the line.

"Well," he says, "What did you learn?"

"Never should have told you about my date with Aaron," Shira responds. "That's what, Ari."

Silence.

"You didn't really expect me to interrogate Aaron right off the bat, did you? Without so much as a howdy-do?" Shira goes on.

"Kind of," Ari answers honestly. "I'm certainly not interested in you falling for the guy again, by the way."

"It may be too late," she responds. "He's a very nice guy."

"The best spies always are," he counters.

"Like you, Ari?"

"I'm the exception that proves the rule," he counters.

"Seriously, Ari. I'm not going to be able to get him to open up—" Shira explains. "—without opening up myself. I have to earn his trust again."

"Like sleeping with him?"

"That's one way. But no. I need to share a few things with him, that's all."

"Well, clear it all with me first," Ari orders her.

Shira is convinced Aaron couldn't possibly be the spy Ari claims he is. Which, granted, makes her a less than objective judge and juror. But she'll do her best.

Yes, she thinks, *he's been friendly with a few Arabs through the years. It's part of his job. But, down deep, he's as patriotic as she is. He believes strongly in Israel's right to exist. He knows, and has felt, the prejudice and pain of persecution that has afflicted all Jews. Like her, all he wants is a little respect.*

But here's the thing. Shira doesn't really know what Aaron believes about some pretty basic stuff. She's making a lot of assumptions. And it's amazing that, in all of their late night conversations, they haven't discussed their core beliefs much at all. At least lately.

Religion? Not something very important to either of them. The Holocaust? Studied. And discussed some. But not something that had much impact on them, in the same way it did their parents. History? They're living it. No time to read about it.

If there's been a constant theme to their conversations, it's been Aaron's steadfast belief that, given enough negotiating, a deal can be made. That, at some level, people want the same things. You just have to be skillful enough to find a way to make both sides relatively happy.

Which, of course, contrasts sharply with Shira's belief that peace for Israel will only come only through force or guile. Nobody will just agree to give up something without pressure. Especially the Arabs.

As Shira thinks about it, the next few days with Aaron could prove interesting.

****

Aaron is a little confused by the attention he's getting all of a sudden from his former girlfriend.

Even back when their relationship was close, there was something coy about how Shira behaved. When she was with him, she was fully engaged. That's for sure. But nobody could disengage as quickly. Here one minute, gone the next.

It was as if she lived her life in chapters, and when she was done with one chapter, she closed it, and started fresh later, with the next one, without looking back.

But, now, for once, Aaron feels like the chapters are flowing together, and he's finally reading the whole book. They have breakfast together. Often, she meets him for lunch. And, in an even more amazing transformation, she prepares dinner for him occasionally. Exotic meals. From places they've both only read about it in books.

She's become quite interested in what he does too, although for the life of him, he can't figure out why. Most would find his daily life incredibly boring.

After years working for groups that were focused on improving Jewish-Muslim relationships, Aaron has segued into a different but tangential line of work. He's now a trade/manufacturing rep for a number of Israeli businesses who do business all over the Middle East.

So, other than the occasional trip to close a deal or something, Aaron just sits in his office and reviews the flow of mostly technical and medical equipment going in and out of Israel, looking for opportunities for his clients.

Admittedly, it's not very exciting. Except when a large purchase is imminent, or a contract comes up for renewal, requiring him to alert his clients and help them develop a strategy.

Actually, it's still not that exciting. Not like what he used to do, that's for sure.

But Aaron's past experience working directly with Arab government officials, and top executives from companies in Muslim countries has proven invaluable to him in his current position. And he makes it a point to stay in touch with as many of his old contacts as possible, even if it's only to get information and referrals.

That's what he intends to do in Cairo this week. Nothing other than rekindle a few relationships, schmooze a little, shake a few hands. So, he's surprised at Shira's interest.

"Who are you meeting with?" she asks.

"Nobody you would know," Aaron says. "Mohammed Pasha is his name. He used to work in a low-level position at the Ministry of Trade but, since Mubarak came into power, he's been doing the same kind of work I do."

"Which is?"

"Putting company executives together and facilitating international trade," Aaron answers.

Sounds pretty vague, Shira thinks. *Could Ari be right?*

"Actually, I just sell stuff. Like you," he says with a grin.

Thirty minutes after Aaron gets into a cab bound for the airport, Shira drives down to Mossad headquarters to meet with Ari. She needs guidance on what is turning out to be a trickier operation than she anticipated.

"He's going to Cairo to meet with somebody named Mohammed Pasha," she reports. "Do you know who that is?"

"No. Our source never mentioned that name."

"Who is your source?"

"Somebody who was part of Sadat's negotiating team during the Camp David meetings," Ari answers.

"Interesting. And why would somebody that high up even know who Aaron is?" Shira asks.

"Actually—" Ari hesitates, then continues, "He knew him because Aaron was there as well, as part of Begin's team. Our source said that, at those meetings, he passed on information about Israel's strategy to a member of the Egyptian delegation."

"Wow," Shira reacts. "Aaron was there? And passed on information. That's big—and damning—and hard to believe."

"We thought so, too," Ari responded. "You see now why I called you back from the Sudan. Who better to sort the situation out? Right?"

"What do you want me to do?" she asks.

"When do you expect Aaron to return?"

"Tomorrow night," Shira answers. "I'm supposed to pick him up at the airport. Then, we're going to stop for dinner somewhere on the way home."

"OK," Ari responds. "You pick the place and let us know where it is. I'll have eyes on you the whole time you're with him. In the meantime, we need to find out what we can about Mohammed Pasha, and about Aaron's role at Camp David. I'll send anything of interest along to you."

"Do you want me to wear a wire?"

"That won't be necessary. We'll figure out some way to have ears on the conversation," Ari answers, "but we may need you to be armed."

"You've got to be kidding," Shira says. "Aaron's a pussy cat. He wouldn't harm anybody, especially me."

"If we're right, Shira, and I think we are, you don't really know Aaron at all."

"I'm betting you're the ones who don't know him," she replies, "but I'm not carrying a gun, no matter what."

"Did you forget that I'm the one who gives orders around here?"

Ari asserts himself, as much as a guy five and a half foot tall can, then continues, "And I can't risk my number one asset becoming collateral damage."

"Listen, Ari," Shira responds. "I've never carried a gun and I'm not going to start now. Besides, I don't have a single outfit in my closet that would hide one."

"All right. But I'm going to be close by, and armed."

"You, Ari? You've got to be kidding."

"You act as if I've never done anything like this before," Ari replies indignantly, "and frankly, I don't trust anybody else to protect you. I've got a vested interest in making sure you come through this operation in one piece."

Shira stands up, comes around the desk and dramatically plants a kiss on Ari's ample cheek.

"That's so sweet of you," she says sarcastically.

The materials arrive as Ari promised. There are two small boxes containing several file folders and documents, enough to keep Shira occupied for a few hours.

The first few folders are about Mohammed Pasha. A quick review shows him to be a highly-respected, well-educated diplomat and later in life, a businessman. In both careers he attended some of the same conferences Aaron did but, as far as Shira can tell, there's no evidence that they ever worked together on anything.

The last few folders are more interesting, especially the papers outlining the events leading up to the September, 1978, meeting at Camp David.

Much of the information was public at the time, and Shira remembers some of the events well.

At the beginning of his presidential term, U.S. President Carter tried to revive a peace process based on the Geneva Peace Conference that had been held before he was elected. There were three objectives of that conference: One, the recognition of Israel's right to exist. Two, Israel's withdrawal from occupied territories. And three, an undivided Jerusalem.

Despite devoting a lot of time and political capital toward reviving it, Carter was making no progress and Anwar Sadat became frustrated. So, on November 9 1977, he announced to his parliament that he intended to go to Israel and speak to the Knesset himself.

As Shira reads, the materials start to get more personal, and confidential. It turns out Aaron was a junior member of the Israeli delegation who met secretly with Sadat on his trip to Israel. Although the President's speech was a consequential event, nothing of substance was discussed with the delegation, and Aaron's role was minor.

Still, Shira is shocked to learn that Aaron's job of "bringing Arabs and Jews together," as he put it at the time, was being performed at such a high level. At the same time she was hiding her new job from Aaron, he was hiding an even bigger government job from her.

But that isn't all. Reading further, she learns that, in the interest of forging their own peace deal, Begin and Sadat decided that a direct dialogue would be helpful and toward that end, they devised a "liaison" scheme where a representative of the Israeli government would be placed in the American embassy in Cairo. His job would be to facilitate direct communication between the two leaders.

They both wanted somebody who wasn't well-known in diplomatic circles, could be trusted by both sides, and could blend easily into the U.S. embassy staff.

And, shockingly, Aaron was on the short list to be that liaison person.

Later, President Carter nixed the idea, probably because he didn't trust the two men to negotiate on their own, with no input from the United States.

Still, how ironic is it that Shira didn't know anything about what Aaron was doing at the time? She was so concerned about hiding her day job that she paid no attention to his more public one.

Skipping ahead to the relevant parts of the Camp David meetings, she confirms that Aaron was, indeed, part of the Israeli negotiating team that accompanied Begin to America. He was actually on the support team assisting Defense Minister, Ezer Weissman, but he didn't seem to play a major role in the negotiations. Or at least not big enough for him to be mentioned in the documents.

In the second box of papers, she found the most meaningful document, a letter from Osama El-Baz, a senior advisor to President Sadat, claiming that Aaron had passed on information "extremely helpful" to their cause.

When Shira finishes her review of the papers, she takes some time to reflect on what she's just learned:

On one hand, how could I be so incurious about Aaron at the time? Here I was thinking that my job was so big and important to the future of Israel that I couldn't share it with Aaron. While he was talking to Begin about how to achieve peace in the Middle East.

What's more surprising is that I didn't even know he held an important position in the Israeli government. And I'm supposed to be trained as a spy. On the other hand, he didn't know much about my activities either. We were both remarkably into our own thing and uninterested in what the other might be doing.

For us, it was a simple arrangement. We liked the freedom. We liked the sex. We liked the banter. But neither of us was committed enough to inquire about what the other was really doing. It just didn't interest us.

Although, if I'm being totally honest, I was the one who set the rules. Aaron was just accepting my terms for the relationship.

****

Shira glances around the dimly-lit cafe, half-expecting Ari to be somewhere within eyesight. But, like any good spy, he's nowhere to be seen. She's glad, because, although she's sure Aaron doesn't know who Ari is, it's best not to risk him recognizing her boss.

There are a few unfamiliar faces sprinkled here and there. Most look suspiciously like they are Mossad agents. Especially the two burly, jowly guys in the corner. They're slouched over an undersized table sipping what appear to be sissy drinks, and trying to avoid eye contact with all of the other diners.

They're probably the ones that will come over and make the arrest, she thinks, *although she's never known the Mossad to work that way. Too bold.*

The table beside them is empty and surprisingly close. It could be where the bug is hidden, either in the small vase of flowers, or under the tablecloth.

Aaron is prattling on about people he met on the trip and a potential deal that might come out of it when Shira decides to cut to the main event right away.

"So, tell me about Camp David," she says abruptly.

"What do you want to know?" Aaron answers without a second of hesitation. He seems guiltless.

"Did you meet President Carter?"

"Not really. I saw him several times from afar," he says. "I did meet Sadat though, and Begin, of course."

"Why didn't you tell me that at the time?"

"I don't know. You didn't seem interested, and I was afraid it might cross a line.'

"What line?"

"The one you drew around your job," he answers. "You made it clear that shop talk was off limits."

"Well, now I'm interested."

"Me, too. About you. I want to know what you've been doing as well."

They look at each other, their eyes locked in dead-eyed stares, then, they both begin to laugh. No matter how serious the conversation gets, their shared sense of humor can always melt the ice, somehow.

"I'll start," Aaron says, the grin still on his face.

"Please," Shira responds.

Her smile has now disappeared. What Aaron is about to say could change their lives forever. And she's not sure she wants that.

"Well," he starts. "I was pretty idealistic, as you might remember. Thought I could change the world through logic and reason."

"I remember."

"I started out arranging meetings between Arabs and Jews in Jerusalem," Aaron continues, "I worked for a non-profit jointly financed by both sides. My job was to contact the leaders of groups with like interests and get them together to talk. Mostly, we discussed their areas of interest. We stayed away from religion and politics for obvious reasons."

"What was the purpose, then?" Shira asks.

"To build a solid foundation for branching into more controversial areas," Aaron explains, "but only when the groups were ready to do so."

"Did it work?"

"I believe so," he says. "Some of the groups are still meeting. I even go occasionally."

"So how did you get into government?"

"I was recruited into the Foreign Ministry to help arrange and facilitate meetings between Israel and our allies," Aaron says matter-of-factly. "Then, after a while, our adversaries."

"What did you do at Camp David?" She asks.

"I prepared briefing papers, researched questions," he answers, "and even sat in on a few rehearsals while Begin reacted to situations that might come up."

"Did you ever do any negotiating of your own?"

"Heavens no. I was way too far down the food chain to engage with Sadat personally."

"How about any of his advisors?" she asks.

Aaron is surprised by the question and looks at Shira suspiciously. Obviously, she's struck a nerve. He sighs as if to say to himself, *Time to come clean. No more beating around the bush.*

"Actually, I did meet with one of Sadat's advisors several times. Just the two of us," Aaron replies. "But I wasn't negotiating. I was more like a conduit to feed stuff to them."

"Why did you do that?"

"My boss, Ezer Weissman, wanted me to do it," Aaron said. "Some of what I passed on was legitimate information about where we were going to hold firm, and where we might give a little. But some of it was just misinformation designed to disguise our real intent."

"So, you were like a spy?"

"More like a double agent. I'm not sure what they believed or didn't believe. But I was working for Mr. Weissman the whole time."

"And our government knew that?" she asks.

"Of course," Aaron answers. "Ezer Weissman was our Defense Minister at the time. He knew everything. Why do you ask?"

"No reason. Just curious, I guess."

****

Shira is once again outside Ari Lavon's office waiting to be invited in. There are several men huddled around his desk discussing something important. At least, it seems that way, based on their serious, pinched faces and loud voices.

Finally, they quiet down and Ari comes out to get her.

"Shira, please come in. We were just discussing you and Aaron," he says. "We have some questions to ask."

"So do I," she responds.

After introductions, Ari compliments Shira on how competently she handled the interrogation of her boyfriend the night before. There are nods of agreement all around. Shira sees but doesn't really acknowledge.

Clearly, there's more to come.

"But we're confused about something," Ari explains. "There's no record anywhere of Ezer Weissman asking Aaron to contact Osama El-Baz during the Camp David meetings. Not in any of the notes, nor in any of our agency's write ups. And, frankly, we think Aaron may have been lying to you about that."

"Why would he do that?"

"To cover his tracks, obviously," says one of the other men. "He probably sniffed out your intent and was covering his ass as best he could. That's what any good spy would do."

"What did Weissman say about Aaron?" Shira counters.

"We haven't talked to him yet. But we have a call in and expect to hear back from him shortly," Ari answers.

"You haven't talked to him yet?" Shira asks in an incredulous tone, and rising from her chair as she speaks. "I can't believe that, Why the hell not?"

"He's a busy man," another man responds. "We really don't want to bother him unless we have a legitimate reason to do so."

"Oh, really?" Shira says. "And yet, you hauled me all the way back here, from an important assignment, and ordered me to interrogate Aaron, all because you'd rather not bother the incredibly important Mr. Weissman?"

"Remember, Shira," Ari says in a calm voice that only infuriates her more. "We didn't know about Weissman until Aaron brought his name up."

"Bullshit. You knew Aaron reported to him. That should have been your first call."

Just at that opportune moment, Ari's phone rings. So, turning his back to the others, he covers his mouth a little and answers it.

For several minutes he says nothing but "I understand," or "yes, sir," and hangs up. Then, Ari turns around, faces

Shira, and says, "Well, that was Mr. Weissman. He finally returned my call."

"And?"

"You were right. Not only did he confirm Aaron's story but he said the young man probably deserves a medal for what he did."

"Isn't that interesting?" Shira responds.

"So, Shira," Ari says with a big smile on his face. "You should be happy. The guy you're dating isn't an enemy spy after all. In fact, he's a hero."

"You think that makes me happy, Ari? I never thought otherwise, remember. So, the question is, does it make you happy?" Shira replies.

Wisely, Ari remains quiet.

So, she just shakes her head and says, "You know what, Ari? I'm tired of you screwing around with me. How can I work with you if you don't trust my judgment? I should just quit this bullshit job once and for all, and get on with my real life."

Ari looks at the other men in disbelief. Surely, she can't be serious.

Shira gets up, then turns to leave, but stops at the door, looks back, and gives her mentor an exaggerated smile.

"And, thank you for making things crystal clear," she says. "You said, I should be happy that Aaron isn't a spy. What I'm really happy about is that, as of now, I'm no longer one. Goodbye, Ari."

Then she leaves, shutting the door behind her.

Epilogue

After her anger subsides, and her judgement returns, Shira reflects on all that's happened to her in her relatively short career as a Mossad agent.

She thinks about her male victims, the relatively harmless men she "seduced" into sharing their secrets with her.

And the Kahn family who trusted her implicitly, and may still to this day.

She thinks about Madame Bacos, the woman she blatantly impersonated, in order to free the Jewish hostages.

And the prostitute who worked with her in Paris, and was later murdered for her troubles.

She remembers fondly her team in the Sudan, even Leon, and the hundreds of refugees they saved. That operation made her really proud.

And she thinks about Eliana, her only true friend at the agency.

All in all, Shira concludes that she probably did more good than bad in her short career. But it's a close call.

On balance though, she has no regrets. Her work in medicine will be more rewarding, if only because the scales lean more toward doing good in the world.

There isn't as much nuance in doctoring, she tells herself. *You either make the patient healthy again, or not. I like that kind of moral clarity.*

That night, after one of their better lovemaking sessions, Aaron sits up in bed, turns toward Shira and says, "So. I've told you everything about me. Now it's your turn to talk, sweetheart."

"OK, what do you want to know?"

"Everything, from the beginning. Let's start with what you do?"

So, Shira sits upright in bed, straightens her pillow behind her head, and begins—

"This may take a while. You remember back when we first met, when we were both students at Hebrew University; well, I was introduced to this little gnome of a man—"

When she finally finishes her long over-due confessional, Aaron says nothing for a few minutes. Then, he sits up, pulls his pillow up behind his head, turns toward her, and looks adoringly into her big, brown eyes.

"I suspicioned that you were doing something pretty secret, and suspicious," he says. "But, the Mossad. Wow. Honestly, I didn't see that one coming."

"Well, I'm not with them anymore. I quit today," Shira says.

"Really? Why?" he asks.

"I had no choice," she answers. "They thought you were a traitor, Aaron. How could I trust them again?"

"They're the Mossad. Nobody trusts them," he says.

Then, Aaron gets a funny look on his face. Finally, he smiles and leans over close to Shira, and whispers. "But they're on our side. And they're really bad ass. And, frankly, given what you just told me, so are you."

"Maybe I should reconsider."

"Maybe you should."